# Somewhere Between Here and Heaven:

## Love's Story

Written by Jovan Roseboro

A Roseboro Consulting Production

Published by
A Roseboro Consulting Production

ISBN-13:

Graphic Design by Robert Crewe
Editing by Adrienne Michelle Horn
Photography by Raymond and Kyla Green

Library of Congress Control Number

Printed in the United States of America

A Roseboro Consulting Production

# Table of Contents

To: Lola

Love You, Fam!!!

*[signature]*

# Foreword

In my latter years when I am faced with the question of why this novel was such a protracted endeavor, I will simply say that I was afraid of how the world would receive such an extraordinary narrative from the depths of the imagination of a G.E.D recipient.

Furthermore, my state of affairs throughout these tumultuous past few years haven't necessarily been financially rewarding, but I continued to strive toward my goal. The people who have grown to know me will tell you that I wrote this in an effort to finance the feeding and clothing of the homeless. Although this is very true, there is an even more honest, intimate reason for publishing this work. For the past five years, the thought of this story has visited me each night in my dreams. I attempted to dismiss the idea, but from beginning to end (and everywhere in between) my mind was plagued with its convoluted details.

GOD, although my heart has smiled over a million times on this journey, nothing has ever given me more joy than fulfilling the tasks that You have placed in my heart. I would ask why it has been so hard, but I believe my beloved Christian community would oppose to me questioning You. Thank You for placing this story in my heart.

Finally, my prayer is that my future children and descendants will overlook that I dropped out of school at sixteen, sold crack cocaine, and committed a long list of other atrocious acts before I embarked on a purpose driven journey to help others. When you hear my personal story, I am confident that you will be extremely proud of my transformation and my efforts. My last wish is that you will engrave I Loved on my tombstone after I have died and ensure that this story is passed down to the many generations to come. Deon would really love that.

# Chapter 1. The Burden of Love

*Does God still answer the prayers we prayed before we die? Or do those prayers even matter anymore?*

As soon as Deon said Amen, the tears began to flow from his eyes. Mrs. Minnie was almost finished praying when she heard his light sniffles from across the kitchen table. As inconsistent as the mid-February warm-today-chilly-the-next-day weather had been that year, she figured that maybe he was coming down with a cold. A few seconds later she said Amen and opened her eyes in time enough to see Deon wiping away tears as he quickly got up to grab a paper towel from the counter behind his chair.

Eight-year-old Deon and his grandmother would pray together every morning. As soon as he would wake up, he would hurry downstairs to the kitchen where his grandmother would already be up cooking

1

breakfast for him, his older brother, Bryce, and older sister, Alexia. He would always sit on the same side of the table to pray as Mrs. Minnie would the other. They would always start silently at the same time, but end aloud on Amen. Deon's Amen always seemed to come before Mrs. Minnie's.

"What's wrong baby?" she asked.

"Nothing," Deon quickly replied as he wiped his face dry.

She knew something was really bothering him because he just stood there staring out the window above the counter. He was attempting to get himself together, but he couldn't hold it. He burst into tears again and quickly began wiping his soft face.

Mrs. Minnie was wise. She knew Deon didn't want to let her see him crying, but she also knew that he wanted to talk about something; otherwise, he would have left the kitchen. She walked over to the stove to stir the big pot of grits she had began cooking earlier that morning.

"Deon, you know you can talk to me about it, but I understand. You're an eight-year-old man now, and…"

2

"Grandma, you'll kill me if I talk to you about it and I'll go to hell. I'm just a kid. I don't want to get killed!" Deon flopped back down into his chair and glowered at the wall.

"Get killed!?!? What in the world are you talking about boy?" she asked as she quizzically stared back at the troubled boy while stirring the grits.

"You promise you won't get mad at me?" he asked.

"Deon, I promise. What's wrong?" Mrs. Minnie replied as she calmly walked back to the table and sat down in front of him.

"He burned down a whole city and killed a bunch of people, drowned a whole bunch of people, and then turned around and killed his own son! He's going to get mad and start killing again! I don't know about you, but I'm scared. Please don't be mad at me Grandma."

By this time, Mrs. Minnie was extremely confused.

"I told you about staying up watching that crazy stuff on TV, Deon. Who are you talking about? I haven't seen anything on the news or in the paper about a killer on the loose," she said while smiling at him.

"I'm talking about GOD, Grandma! If He's such a good man, why did He kill all those people and His own Son?" Deon asserted.

Mrs. Minnie's jaw dropped in amazement as she looked across the table. She couldn't believe what she had just heard her grandson say. She wasn't mad at him at all. In fact, she was quite impressed at how precocious he was becoming. His little mind was constantly thinking about things that most would say were far beyond his years.

He was the epitome of inquisitiveness. Deon asked questions for a reason. He always wanted to figure things out on his own. There's a very good chance his brilliant mind will lead him to endure things no young man should experience too early in life, and if it does, Deon will be fine.

"Deon, God is good. When Jesus died on the cross, didn't He come back?" Deon nodded his head in agreement as he eagerly waited on his grandmother to continue. Mrs. Minnie knew that she would need to explain further, as always. The beauty of Deon's unsatisfied mind made her heart smile. It also kept her thinking.

"Well think about it Deon. Who do you think let Him rise up again? When He burned those people up, weren't they doing bad things?"

"But Grandma there had to be kids there when He burned them people up and when He flooded everything. Kids is just kids. They can't help it that the old people was acting the fool. So if He gets mad at them people up the street selling drugs, what's gonna happen to us?"

"You don't have to worry about anything baby. When God sent Jesus to the cross, He died so that God wouldn't have to do any of those things anymore."

Mrs. Minnie got up and went back to the stove knowing that Deon was pondering every word that she had just spoken, but refused to say anything else.

Time is the best teacher. She was simply allowing him to grow up. He sat there for a few moments tending to his racing thoughts, before he ran upstairs to wake his brother and sister.

Lord, help me with this boy, she quietly said to herself as she finished cooking and set the table. Mrs. Minnie and her grandchildren ate breakfast together every morning. Mrs. Minnie was the fifty-eight-year-old widow of Mr. Harry Lennon. He died twenty-two years ago at the young age of thirty-eight, peacefully in his sleep right beside Mrs. Minnie. For years, it was rumored that Mrs. Minnie killed him. That was primarily because Mr. Harry Lennon was a handsome mahogany-skinned, black man, and Mrs. Minnie was a beautiful ivory-skinned white woman. The autopsy revealed that he died of natural causes, but in rural Whiteville, North Carolina where the few provincials in the area spread rumors out of something to do; some of the residents have always believed that Mrs. Minnie killed him for his insurance money.

They met when she was in her freshmen year of college at the University of North Carolina Wilmington, about an hour east of town. Mr. Harry Lennon was a young, successful insurance salesman at the time who worked in Downtown Whiteville. He had been an usher in his church since he was a small child. Every Sunday, he was the first person members saw when they walked into the sanctuary. He was a cute, slender, brown-skinned child who was happy to greet everyone with a church program and a warm spirit. He embodied what those in his community would call good Southern hospitality. Mr. Harry Lennon always smiled. His smile was surely the whitest smile most had ever seen, and went perfectly with his charm.

Mrs. Minnie will be forever grateful to her Whiteville-native, college roommate, Karen McKinney, who took the responsibility of making sure that she and Mr. Harry Lennon remained love birds until the end of time. Years ago, Mrs. Minnie had decided to spend one weekend with Karen's family. It was tradition for them to attend church service every Sunday. When Mr. Harry Lennon and Mrs. Minnie saw each other that morning when they went to church, it was love at first sight. She was a tall, curvaceous woman who stood a little over six feet in her most decent pair of heels. Her head full of orphan Annie red hair coupled with her flawless ivory skin proved to be an appreciated sight for most men. She walked rather sultry, but prided herself in not acting anything less than a lady should.

Throughout the early stages of their relationship, they both confided in Karen when they had problems with one another. She quickly became Mrs. Minnie's excuse to come visit Mr. Harry Lennon in Whiteville and, of course, Mr. Harry Lennon's excuse to go visit Mrs. Minnie at UNCW. The idea of interracial dating wasn't widely accepted at that time, especially along the Bible Belt of the Jim Crowe South.

Those two were as inseparable as they could be, granted the circumstances. Every weekend and a few times throughout the course of each week, those love birds made sure that they were together. In the beginning, they were secretive about their romance. But soon it became impossible not to tell the truth when all of the time they were spending together came into question. As fate would have it, Mrs. Minnie discovered that she was pregnant with the first and only life they would ever create, Love. Mrs. Minnie hadn't told her parents about Mr. Harry Lennon up until this point. She had very good reason not to.

Mrs. Minnie grew up watching how her parents treated their farmhands. Her father, Mr. Michael Riggs, inherited his family's lucrative tobacco farms in Smithfield as soon as he graduated from high school. Her mother, Mrs. Amy, was the typical Southern housewife. They were extremely unkind to the help, most of which consisted of the Blacks and Mexicans. As a child, Mrs. Minnie dreaded the idea of becoming an integral part of her father's tobacco empire. That would mean that she would live the remainder of her life as a country girl on a farm. She believed that singing would be her only way out, but not if she would be forced to sing that country music her mother had urged her to sing since she was a small girl. Her voice was as angelic as anyone else's, but she had a passion for Rhythm &Blues. Her father hired a singing coach and entered her into all of the talent shows, but when she began her first year of high school, she refused to sing anything that was not in the genre of her passion. Her decision insulted her parents and they made the decision to stop supporting her dream.

Her singing instructor tried her best to convince her parents to let Mrs. Minnie sing the R&B styled music that she loved. Shortly after her suggestion, she was told that her services were no longer needed. Mrs. Minnie stopped singing around her parents completely after that time. She saw it as a way to punish her parents, who had dearly loved to hear her sing. Her audience quickly dwindled to the farmhands that worked the fields behind their home and her friends at school.

The farmhands would take their daily breaks at the open-walled tin shed not too far from the Riggs' home, right at the edge of the family owned tobacco field. Their brick, ranch-styled home sat in the middle of a beautifully landscaped two-acre yard surrounded by acres of the inherited cash crop fields. When Mrs. Minnie was in middle school, her father entrusted her to drive his old pick-up truck to bring cold sodas and Nekot nabs for the workers each day during the summer on their lunch break. As soon as she hopped into the truck, she would turn the radio to the local R&B station and sing to her heart's content. There was not one song she didn't know the words to. After distributing the goods to the workers, Mrs. Minnie would always put on a mini-concert for them. Her voice was the highlight of their day. It would always put them in a good mood. They enjoyed every minute of it and eagerly looked forward to her return each day. Mrs. Minnie followed this same routine for years and never became bored with it. Unbeknownst to her, Mr. Riggs had known for years what Mrs. Minnie was doing for the workers at the shed, but he didn't mind it at all. He was paying them less than minimum wage, and was willing to do whatever it took to keep them working in his fields. Mrs. Amy, however, didn't like it at all. On more than one occasion she mentioned to Mr. Riggs that she didn't feel comfortable with the way that some of the workers looked at her and Mrs. Minnie when they went out in the yard to work. The truth is that they could have cared less about the uppity, old woman. Mrs. Minnie was intelligent enough to realize that her mother did not like black people. She would commonly refer to the farmhands as the niggers in most of her conversations with Mr. Riggs.

As a child, Mrs. Amy would never have an issue with Mrs. Minnie's white friends spending time at the house, but could always find an excuse whenever Mrs. Minnie asked if her black friends could come over as well. She was around the same age as some of the farmhands' children and went to the same school as many of them. They were indeed considered to be some of her best friends, and they were thankful that she grew up to be nothing like her parents.

Mrs. Minnie felt like her parents treated the farmhands very much like slaves. She loved her parents dearly, but was hurt by the fact that they were so mean-hearted. She rebelled by refusing to sing in their presence, to participate in any extra-curricular activities at school, and to do anything extra that would make them excessively proud of her. Her father knew the true origin of her discontent, but was far too concerned with his profits to care about treating the farmhands any better. They were never paid over minimum wage. Never. Not even those who had been dedicated to working on the farm for over a decade.

After graduating from high school, Mrs. Minnie went to college and majored in Education. To be honest, she really wasn't enthusiastic about going, but it proved to be an opportunity to separate herself from her parents and that wretched farm life she had become so adjusted to. For the first time in her life she felt free. That feeling was all the encouragement she needed to be great. It motivated her to maintain a 4.0 GPA, become involved in as many student activities as she could, and even take a chance at singing again. She sang in the choir at the church that she and Karen McKinney attended a few blocks away from campus. She rarely visited home and made sure she told her parents that she was busy when they offered to visit. Although she still loved them, she felt as though it would be in her best interest to stay as far away as she could for as long as she could.

As for Mr. Harry Lennon, both of his parents were preachers. His father was the pastor at Whiteville Baptist Church (the church where he and Mrs. Minnie met) for many years. His mother would preach there occasionally as well. Although Mr. Harry Lennon was their only child, they had willingly housed many children from the area who had issues in their own homes. Most of those children had the unfortunate luck of being birthed to drug addicts or uncaring parents. Mr. Harry Lennon's parents both had the gift of working with troubled youth. There must have been five to six new children who came to the Lennons' house each year. Many compared it to a boot camp. The Lennons took in some of the worst behaved children, but would completely transform each one of them by the time they were dismissed to live in the world on their own. Whatever Mr. Harry Lennon's parents were doing with those children worked. It was indeed magical.

Mr. Harry Lennon was one who most people would consider the perfect child. He was incredibly smart and always eager to help others whenever he could. He would mow the lawns of senior citizens in the neighborhood without charging them one penny. Everyone in Whiteville loved and respected him. Instead of going to college, he chose to get his insurance license and become an agent at the small insurance company downtown, Marley Insurance. When the elderly people in Whiteville whose lawns he had cut found out that he was an insurance agent, they made sure that they were the first ones in line to sign up for a policy. Not too long after, members of his father's church and his former school teachers came to get a policy also. Being a kindhearted gentleman all those years made Mr. Harry Lennon one of the most successful insurance agents in the eastern part of the state very quickly. Regardless of how much money he made, he still ushered in church every single Sunday morning.

When Mrs. Minnie became pregnant with Love, it took her a little over a month to build up enough courage to tell her parents. She was more afraid of telling them that she was pregnant by a black man than she was of telling them that she was pregnant at all. And rightfully so. Mr. Harry Lennon was the perfect man. He was young, successful, and had a future brighter than most men his age, but his skin color would have been thought to horrify her parents at the least.

When she broke the news to Mrs. Amy over the phone, it went a lot better than she thought it would have initially. Mr. Riggs wasn't home when she called. Mrs. Amy was surprisingly excited at first. She had always wanted grandchildren, but then she posed the ultimate question to Minnie during that call.

"Who's the father, Minnie?"

After mentally preparing herself for her mother's reaction, she began explaining that he was a handsome, God-fearing, successful insurance agent who was a gentleman beyond anything she could have ever imagined. Finally, she became confident enough to do one of the most courageous things she had ever done in her life – tell her mother that the father of her child was a black man.

Suddenly, there was a moment of silence on the phone between them. What happened next will forever be one of the most memorable moments in Mrs. Minnie's life.

"Minnie do you love him?"

"Yes," Mrs. Minnie replied as resolutely as she had ever spoken to her mother. She freed herself in that moment. No more hiding. No more being afraid of what her parents might think.

Mrs. Amy began to cry. It wasn't hard for Mrs. Minnie to realize that these weren't tears of joy.

"I don't know how to feel right now, Minnie. We gave you the world and you just seem like you won't ever be satisfied. We let you make your own decisions, and other than supporting your dreams of wanting to sing that god-awful music, we've always

17

given you the best, young lady. If you really love this man I understand, but do you really know what this means?" Mrs. Amy said with a bit of anger.

"Mama, I love him. And I'm going to love this baby! You and daddy ain't got to like it! What do you mean 'Do I know what this means?!?'" Mrs. Minnie screamed.

"Now don't you talk to me like that Minnie Riggs. You're young, dumb, and just don't use your brain, child. You have no idea how hard it is raising a baby. And you sho' ain't got a damn clue how hard it's gonna be raising a nigger baby!" Mrs. Amy cried out. Before Mrs. Minnie could respond, her mother slammed the phone down on the hook.

Mrs. Amy was devastated. She cried and paced through that house for hours after she hung up the phone. It was much more than Mrs. Amy thought she could handle. Late that night when Mr. Riggs walked into their home, he called for his wife, but there was no answer. He looked all over for her, but could not find her. When he made his way to the phone to call the neighbors to see if she had come by, there was an envelope with his name on

18

it propped against a lamp on the nightstand. Before he picked up the phone to call, he opened the letter and started reading.

*Michael,*

*I love you with all my heart. You gave me a life that most women only dream about and I found a way to mess all of it up. It's been over 15 years and you haven't looked at me the same. That night was about me. I was mad. I was selfish. I was...young, Michael. I gave you my heart. I know I disappointed you. Hell, I know it took a piece of you that I never got back. All I've ever wanted to do was give you that piece of you back. I'm sorry. Minnie called today and gave me some news that I am not able to deal with. Your daughter is pregnant by a nigger she is in love with. I have on my best dress and have made my face up already. Tell that daughter of yours that I love her, but I can't live knowing she's one of them. You take care, Michael Riggs. This is what I have to do. You will find that woman. You deserve so much more than*

19

*anything I could have ever grown to be. They say this is what cowards do. Michael, I am a coward. You'll find me in the field behind the house.*

*I Love You. I'm sorry.*

*Amy*

He skimmed over the letter quickly and ran out of the house to the field screaming her name. There, just beyond the shed the farmhands used to take their breaks, her dead body lay. Mrs. Amy had taken her husband's pistol and put a bullet into her brain through her open mouth. He stayed out there crying throughout the night as he stared at her lifeless corpse. He didn't find the strength to call the authorities until the next morning.

In that letter, Mrs. Amy was referring to the short lived relationship she had with another man she had been with during a time where she and Mr. Riggs had marital problems. They got together one weekend while she was visiting her sister in Raleigh. Mr. and Mrs. Riggs were at a difficult point in their marriage. He was always stressed due to the amount of time he invested into the tobacco business, and she seemingly could never do anything that pleased him. They found themselves arguing all of the time. He would stay out extremely late and come home drunk a lot. It was then that all of the lovely compliments he used to shower on her would be replaced with unkind words like ugly and dumb. He had even gone as far as to shout that she wasn't the one for him. Mr. Michael Riggs had succeeded in making Mrs. Amy feel as though she no longer served any purpose in his life.

Mrs. Amy knew very well that she would soon entertain the man she met in Raleigh. She was at her wits end with Mr. Riggs, and the other man lived very close to her sister. They would even cross paths with one another at the gas station and the grocery store every once in a while. He begged Mrs. Amy's sister to give her his phone number so that they could become acquainted with each other. Knowing that Mrs. Amy was enduring one of the hardest times of her marriage, Mrs. Amy's sister gave Mrs. Amy his phone number and begged her to call him. When she became completely frustrated with her situation, she finally picked up the phone and did so. From the first moment they spoke, she knew that their friendship would be something that she would later regret. They made sure that they spoke to each other when Mr. Riggs wasn't at home. One night Mrs. Amy decided that Mr. Riggs had stayed out one too many nights drinking and that she would no longer settle for being called names. A few weeks later, she met the other man in Raleigh and indulged in the most passionate love-making experience she hadn't had in years.

When she made it back to Whiteville, she felt guilty and couldn't go another day without telling her beloved husband. She was sincerely apologetic and suggested that they see a marriage counselor. Once their sessions had ended, Mr. Riggs had stopped drinking, but was never the same. He loved her enough to stay committed to their marriage, but the love never grew into anything greater. For 15 years, the one time she adulterated became the dark cloud over their marriage. Mrs. Amy never forgave herself, and deep within, Mr. Riggs had never forgiven her either. He also never spoke another word to Mrs. Amy's sister. Mrs. Amy desperately wanted to try counseling again throughout the years, but Mr. Riggs refused in efforts not to dig up a memory he so desperately wanted to keep buried. She realized a long time ago how badly she had hurt him. She figured that the bullet would signify that she had brought it all to a close.

Mr. Riggs called his daughter soon after he had contacted the authorities. He was rather calm when he broke the news to her, and did his best to comfort her when she started crying and screaming uncontrollably. He wanted her to come home, and truthfully, she needed to. Regardless of the rather poor relationship she had with her mother, she needed to show her respects to the person who raised her to be a fine young woman. Mr. Riggs insisted that Mr. Harry Lennon drive her home. He knew that Mrs. Minnie was in no condition to drive and he also wanted to meet him. It baffled her as to how her father knew about him, but it didn't matter at that moment. When Mrs. Minnie called Harry and broke the news to him, he immediately rushed to her dorm room to pick her up and head to her parents' home.

Mr. Riggs made it very clear to everyone in the community that he didn't want any visitors that evening. When Mrs. Minnie and Mr. Harry Lennon arrived, they sat in the driveway for a while. Mrs. Minnie had been crying for most of the day and pulling into that driveway immediately worsened her grief.

There wasn't a single light on in the house. Mr. Harry Lennon had assumed that no one was there, but Mrs. Minnie knew that her father would be inside waiting. She would be Mr. Riggs' main concern at this point. When they walked toward the house, Mr. Harry Lennon became deathly afraid of what Mr. Riggs would think of him being with his daughter. As they walked in, Mrs. Minnie hurried over to her father who had fallen asleep on the couch hours earlier. He was awakened by the commotion and quickly sat up to embrace her. They sat on the sofa crying for what seemed like an hour without saying a word. There was no need to.

Mr. Harry Lennon stood just inside the doorway across the room in tears himself. It was a moment where the heaviness of the room weighed upon all of their hearts. After the tears subsided, Mr. Riggs was introduced to Mr. Harry Lennon, who then appropriately offered his condolences. Their meeting was not anything less than pleasant.

Mrs. Minnie could barely hold herself together. She was happy that her father had found a way to accept Mr. Harry Lennon in that moment, but the pain of her mother's suicide was almost unbearable. As Mrs. Minnie sat sobbing, she watched as her father bonded with the future father of her child. Mr. Riggs was rather composed granted the circumstances. When Mrs. Minnie retired for the evening, those two men stayed up for hours becoming acquainted with one another. Not once was the subject of the baby or Mr. Harry Lennon's race mentioned in conversation. Soon Mr. Riggs decided to face the reality that he would go to sleep that night without his wife for the first time in over a decade.

As Mr. Riggs stood up from the sofa and began walking towards the hallway that led to his bedroom, he stopped and stared into Mr. Harry Lennon's eyes. The stare made Mr. Harry Lennon slightly nervous, but he stared back at him just as any true man would.

"Harry, I know you love her; I can feel it. You seem to be a fine young man and I like you. Now I've got to tell you that I've not always been too fond of blacks, and that's just being honest. But, that young lady you got pregnant in there made me realize how wrong I was for not liking people without having a reason. She took her voice away from me. That girl used to walk around this house and sing a smile on me and Amy's face. Didn't really matter what kind of mood we were in. When she sang, it always made it feel good 'round here. I'm pretty sure she told you, but when we stopped taking her to those lessons, the only people that could enjoy that voice were the guys I got working 'round here. They had a piece of my daughter that I couldn't enjoy no more," Mr. Riggs said as he wiped tears from his face.

"You make sure she finishes school. Don't let her think that just because she's going to have a baby that she can just give up and be a housewife. You don't want that, Harry. I know from experience. Let her make mistakes, and when she tells you that she's sorry, don't make her pay for it forever. Learn how to forgive. Don't be like I was." By this time he couldn't stop the tears from flowing from his eyes. Mr. Harry Lennon just sat there and listened. He was too shocked to say anything.

"And Harry, don't go on like this, son. Make it right. If you're brave enough to be with a white lady and get her pregnant, then be brave enough to marry her."

Mr. Riggs gave Mr. Harry Lennon a blanket and pillow and allowed him to sleep on the sofa. He liked Mr. Harry Lennon, but not enough to let him sleep in the same room with Mrs. Minnie under his roof.

They buried Mrs. Amy rather quickly. She had a small funeral that consisted of immediate family members and a few friends. Mrs. Amy never had many friends anyway. Everyone seemed to be more focused on Mr. Harry Lennon and Mrs. Minnie than they were on the funeral. Although most were not pleased with Mrs. Minnie publicly displaying her love for a black man, they found a way in their hearts to accept it. They figured that dealing with the death of her mother was enough in itself without adding their disapproval of what she had chosen to do with her life.

After fifteen years, Mr. Riggs finally spoke to the one person he vowed that he would never speak to again - Mrs. Amy's sister. He walked up to her at the funeral, gave her hug and whispered that he was sorry. And that ended their interaction. There was no need to say anything else.

Mr. Riggs never told anybody about the note Mrs. Amy wrote. Not too long after the funeral, he went back to work. He gave all the farmhands a healthy raise, and

convinced them to get health insurance policies with
Mr. Harry Lennon.

Mrs. Minnie was eight months pregnant when
she walked down the aisle of Whiteville Baptist
Church to marry Mr. Harry Lennon. That was the
largest event to ever be held there. Mr. Riggs, his
farmhands, and each of the bride and groom's
families and friends were all there. Karen McKinney
rightfully served as the Maid of Honor while Mr.
Harry Lennon's parents presided over the ceremony.
It seemed as though everyone in Whiteville came to
witness the momentous occasion. Mrs. Minnie was
glowingly beautiful, even though she was one month
shy of delivering her child.

Everyone had a beautiful time that day. A mixed-
race crowd was rarely seen enjoying moments
together during that time. Mr. and Mrs. Harry Lennon
changed what had been deemed abnormal for so
many years. They made history by becoming the first
interracial couple to be married in the county. It was
the news of the town, and they all gossiped about

how in love they were with one another. One week before Love was born, Mr. Harry Lennon bought a modest two-story home in Whiteville. That little girl was spoiled as soon as she exited her mother's womb and entered the world. When Mr. Riggs received word that Love was born, he raced down to Whiteville and held her in his arms for three consecutive hours. Many friends and family members visited throughout the week, but Mr. Riggs stayed there the four days his first grandchild was in the hospital.

Mrs. Minnie didn't spend much time away from school after she had Love. After a few months, she enrolled again and registered for her classes. Mr. Harry Lennon had more business than he could handle, but never wanted to go into business for himself. Mr. Riggs spent most of his free time down in Whiteville. He couldn't stand to be away from his granddaughter too long. Mrs. Minnie eventually graduated with honors and was hired as an elementary school teacher. Mr. Harry Lennon's success continued to grow over the years.

When Love was about three-years-old, Mr. Riggs did the unthinkable. Since Mrs. Amy's suicide, he never was the same. He went from loving the farming industry to hating everything about it. He sold his home and half of his tobacco business and decided that it would be best if he moved to Whiteville to spend more time with his granddaughter. Mr. Riggs could have sold it all and lived more than comfortable for the rest of his life. He had become very rich over the years from all of the work he put into farming. The only reason he kept a piece of the business is because he wanted to make sure that the farmhands would not be treated poorly. Love never spent a day in daycare once he settled into his new home. Mr. Riggs would go to his daughter's house every morning and babysit his beautiful granddaughter each day until Mrs. Minnie came home from work.

On Sundays, the entire family would go to church together. It was hard to keep Love out of the pulpit when her grandfather was preaching. As soon

31

as she heard his voice, she would run straight to the front of the church and walk towards him. Most of his sermons were delivered with his granddaughter standing beside him. Everyone adored her.

Growing up, Love was Whiteville's little star. She was absolutely gorgeous. She always had a head full of long, soft brunette hair and naturally tanned skin. Love had a very small frame as a child, but the older she became the more she began to look like a model. Everyone in the town always encouraged her to aspire to be one. Those who didn't know her genetic composition thought she was an American Indian. She was truly a Mulatto princess.

She inherited Mrs. Minnie's voice. The first person to notice it was Mr. Riggs. When he would babysit her in her younger years, she would sing along with the songs on her favorite children TV shows. Sometimes listening to his granddaughter forced tears from his eyes as he was reminded of how Mrs. Minnie used to sing and make everyone smile around the house when she was a small girl.

By the time Love was nine-years-old, she was leading songs in the church choir, participating in beauty pageants, cheering on the local squad, and joining almost every extracurricular activity she could get into at school. She was extremely intelligent like her mother and earned A's in all of her classes. Everyone was proud of her.

She loved all of her family, but her father was her hero. Whenever he was off of work, she would be by his side. During the summer, she would ride around with Mr. Harry Lennon collecting insurance payments and writing new policies. She knew more about the insurance business than most people in the Marley Insurance office by the time she was fifteen. He was her heart. When Mr. Harry Lennon died in his sleep, Love had just turned sixteen-years-old. A piece of the beautiful life that she'd grown to love had been taken away from her and would never be given back.

There was a light, constant rain on the day of the funeral. The weather was perfect all week, but on that day, it seemed like the sun never rose. Dark clouds rested between the sun and the earth all day long. Being that Mr. Harry Lennon had become something like a celebrity around the town, the services had to be held at the local community college's auditorium. It easily sat one thousand people, but even that proved to be too small on that rainy day. The mourning of the moment kept tears in their eyes and words in the back of their throats.

Mrs. Minnie sobbed from the time she awakened that morning and sporadically screamed out "Harry" throughout the entire service. Mr. Riggs did the best he could to comfort his daughter as he wiped tears from his own eyes. Love was hurt by her father's passing, but hadn't shed one tear. She sat there on the front row staring at the casket of her hero. There were times where she would close her eyes and think about the happy moments that she spent with her father. At the end of the service when they allowed everyone to view Mr. Harry Lennon's body for the last time, a few tears finally flowed from Love's eyes. She walked up to the casket, kissed Mr.

Harry Lennon on his cheek, and gently placed her hand on the opposite side of her father's face for the last time.

Mrs. Minnie and Mr. Riggs were the last two people to make their pass. As Mrs. Minnie approached, a tight smile peered from beneath her wet smeared make-up and a look of adoration swept across her face while she looked at her knight in shining armor resting peacefully. He had given her more happiness than she could have ever dreamed of having. Now, he was in the one place that he had always talked about going – Heaven. She leaned over, kissed his forehead, and told him for what would be the last time that she loved him.

When Mr. Riggs walked up to Mr. Harry Lennon's casket, he reached in, grabbed Mr. Harry Lennon's shoulder, and said, "You were a better man than I'll ever be Harry. Thank you for changing my life."

The ride to the gravesite was a quiet one. After the ceremony, Love decided to stay a bit longer than everyone else. The gravesite was within walking distance of their home. As the gravediggers did their work, she stood under the tent that was set up for the burial ceremony and stared at her father's plot. She wanted to hold on to a few extra moments with her father before they completely covered that hole. She cried profusely as she watched them work. When they were finished, they offered to give her a ride home, but she refused. Love just wanted some alone time there. She stayed there under that tent for a little more than an hour after they left, and finally walked home alone in the rain.

As she walked through her neighborhood, it seemed like the clouds parted just enough to allow a few rays of sunshine to gently kiss her face. Typically, that would have been enough to put a smile on anyone's face but this was an atypical day. Those few beams of sun just made Love cry more than she had done earlier.

There were dozens of people at the house by the time she arrived. Some waited for her outside on the front porch, while others awaited her inside. When Love walked up they tried to speak to her, but she didn't say a word let alone acknowledge the fact that she was even being addressed. She intentionally walked briskly past the visitors on the porch, and quickly maneuvered her way through the crowd of people inside so that she could make her way upstairs to her bedroom. Love locked her door behind her and lied down on her bed. It was then that she finally felt free to release all of the emotions that were inside of her.

Mr. Riggs saw Love walk into the house. A few moments after she went into her room, he had made his way upstairs and knocked on her door. She didn't respond. All he could do was listen to her muffled cries through the door. Mrs. Minnie walked up the stairs shortly after and saw Mr. Riggs looking out the window at the end of the hallway. She couldn't stand listening to the faint sound of Love crying and seeing her father at the end of the hallway staring out at the clouded-gloomy day. She quickly made her way back downstairs.

Mr. Harry Lennon was an angel to so many people. But the truth is that earth angels can't stay

37

here forever. One day every living soul will have to go home, and those they leave behind have to continue to live. Mrs. Minnie and Mr. Riggs understood that concept all too well. Maybe things would have turned out differently for Love if she would have been able to cope with the loss of her hero.

The rumor that Mrs. Minnie killed Mr. Harry Lennon started floating around town rather quickly. It all began with the workers at Marley Insurance. Mr. Harry Lennon had a healthy insurance policy that was left to be split evenly between only two beneficiaries - his parents' church and Mrs. Minnie. For years his parents refused to let him put them down as beneficiaries on his policy. They were more than comfortable with their lifestyle, and weren't too concerned with matters of money. They insisted that Mr. Harry Lennon give the money to the church if anything ever happened to him. The women at the insurance office couldn't figure out why none of the money was left to his parents. The rumor started as soon as one of the gossiping women jokingly posed the question "I wonder if she killed him?"

Mrs. Minnie and Mr. Riggs started noticing a difference in how people treated them. After the rumor started, the genuine smiles that once filled the church when they walked in were no longer there. Mr. Harry Lennon's parents would always make them feel at home, but others would hardly acknowledge the fact that they were present.

Mrs. Minnie went to the beauty salon every other Saturday to get her hair washed. Most times she and the women would gossip about the happenings of Whiteville. After the rumor, those women hardly said a word when Mrs. Minnie walked in. They would be cordial, but nothing more. The teachers at the elementary school would act the same way in the lounge at work. The same went for Mr. Riggs when he went to the barber shop and to the Donut Shop in the mornings to get his daily cup of coffee. It burdened Mrs. Minnie so much that she stood up in church one Sunday morning during the time they designated for testimonies and told everyone how she felt about the way she had been treated. When she marched her way down the aisle to the front of the church, everyone looked surprised. Every eye in the congregation was fixated on her. As the piano player played soft-moving music, she looked over the crowd and smiled.

"When I first started coming to this church, I felt like I was meant to be here. Y'all never made me feel like I was out of place or any of that. When me and Harry got together y'all never once made us the least bit uncomfortable. And yes it surprised us because of the difference in our skin colors and everything, but we were glad that y'all were able to look past it and see the love that we saw in each other. When Love was born and my father moved down here, y'all gave them the same respect that y'all gave me and Harry. I could feel God in this place from the time I hit the church yard for all these years. Now that Harry is gone, my baby don't come no more. I don't feel that same kind of thing that I felt when I first started coming. The biggest part of my heart other than my daughter, was raised right here in this church. Harry touched everybody in this room. If he was here right now, he would be ashamed of some of you. I

40

overheard one of my students telling some kids that I killed my husband. What kind of foolishness is that? But I know that a kid didn't come up with that idea all by their self. I love you all, and whatever I did to any of you, I ask that you find it in your heart to forgive me." At that point Mrs. Minnie began to cry. She wasn't alone. A lot of people sat with tears in their eyes.

Mr. Harry Lennon's mother left the pulpit with tears in her eyes and walked right over to Mrs. Minnie and hugged her. One by one, members of the congregation followed suit. It was an emotional moment, but Mr. Harry Lennon's father preached from the pit of his soul that day! He spoke about Christians having a responsibility to love one another and to not hurt others by gossiping. It was a sermon that convicted everyone in that room who had treated Mrs. Minnie unkindly. After that day, many of the people of Whiteville started to speak to Mrs. Minnie and Mr. Riggs again, but even with those apologies, some in the town still chose to believe the rumor.

41

Love rarely went to church after her father died. The once vibrant, goal-oriented girl who had led the choir withdrew her warm personality and became cold. She spent most of her time in her cluttered room when she was home. Getting her to speak more than one or two sentences at a time became a task. Mrs. Minnie, Mr. Riggs, and Mr. Harry Lennon's parents tried their best to convince her to see a counselor, but she refused. She begged Mrs. Minnie to let her cope with it in her own way, and she respected daughter's wishes.

Love was one of the prettiest girls at Whiteville High School. Any one of the boys there would have jumped at the chance to be in a relationship with her before her father died had the chance presented itself. Every Valentine's Day since she had been in the sixth grade, she would get at least three dozen roses delivered to the office from secret admirers. Oftentimes, she would find that random letters had been slipped in her locker from boys who were too shy to confront her. She did not pay them any attention. She was more concerned with studying so that she could become successful. Being in a high school

42

relationship was the last thing on her mind. But after her father passed, the heartbreak started to take her over completely. She no longer smiled or engaged others in casual conversation. She only spoke when she was spoken to. She stopped participating in all of her extracurricular activities, but her grades still plummeted. The guidance counselor as well as all of the teachers tried to motivate her to do better. Her blank face brought them to tears sometimes when they tried to reach out to her. Although the other students still liked her, they realized that she was becoming more awkward as the days passed. She was known around school as *the girl who became weird after her dad died*. She became unnoticed and unimportant, until the day he spoke to her.

Diondre Howard was his name. Everyone called him D. The young man had just transferred from Lumberton Senior High School, located about twenty miles away. Since a small boy, Diondre was a star on the football field. Ranked as one of the best quarterbacks in the region, his father felt as though he would have a better chance at receiving a scholarship if he went to Whiteville High. Whiteville, by far, had the best athletic program in the area. They had won numerous state championships, and ever since the coach saw Diondre play in the pre-season of his ninth grade year, he decided that he was going to make him a part of his winning team. Diondre's father worked at a factory in Whiteville, but lived in a Lumberton home that he and Diondre's mother had bought right after Diondre was born. Unfortunately, his mother died in a car accident when Diondre was eight-years-old.

She had gotten into a drunken argument one night with Diondre's abusive father. Alcohol fueled most of their arguments then. His mother threatened to leave him plenty of times, but never did. Usually, she would stay with one of her friends for a few hours to compose herself before returning home. On that rainy night, she took young Diondre with her. She lost control of her car while driving around a curve she knew well. It's a miracle that Diondre survived. Although she had her seatbelt buckled, the trees that rested along the side of the road shattered through the windshield on impact. She lived long enough to tell Diondre that she loved both him and his father. That was the only thing Diondre remembered hearing as he watched her pass away before help could arrive. His father never drank alcohol again after that. Moving to Whiteville so that Diondre could play football on a championship team was the best thing for Diondre and his father. There were too many bad memories in Lumberton, and they were both determined to leave their past there.

When Love went to lunch, she sat in the quietest corner of the cafeteria by herself as she had always done so that no one would disturb her. Diondre usually sat with his teammates and a few other popular people that attended the school at a table that was not too far away from where Love sat. But on this day, Diondre approached her as soon as he paid for his lunch and sat a few seats down from Love. Most people who sat in that area were either studying or isolating themselves from everyone else. Diondre needed to study for the algebra exam that he would be taking next period and had not studied for it at all. Matter of fact, he rarely studied for any other test either. Passing classes was one thing that superstar high school athletes like him never had to be concerned with. As long as they completed most of their assignments, teachers passed them.

Although they had never spoken, Love knew all too well who Diondre was. They had an English class together when he first enrolled into Whiteville High. She didn't even look his way that day when he sat down at her table. He gave her no choice but to acknowledge that he was there once he started speaking to her.

"Love, I don't mean to bother you right now, but by any chance, do you know anything about quadratic equations?"

"No. Not too much. Why?"

"Wow! So you actually speak. That's the first time I've ever heard you say a word." He was indeed surprised. Love continued eating as though she hadn't heard a word he said.

"I was just trying to make small talk. Look, I can't flunk this exam and I have about twenty-five minutes before its staring me right in my face. If you can tell me anything about these quadratic equations, I would be so grateful. Please," Diondre sincerely pleaded.

He wasn't the brightest student in high school by any means. He barely maintained a 2.7 GPA even with the help of the best tutors the booster club could afford and the smartest teenagers in school helping him as much as they could. He was nowhere near having the grades he needed to get into any college with or without a scholarship.

Love had finished eating by that time, and politely moved closer to him to look at the problems he didn't understand. His grades were not low because he didn't try; he just was not as academically gifted as some of his schoolmates. Love helped him as much as she could until the bell sounded for them to go to their classes. Before they left, he stood up and gave her the biggest hug in appreciation for what she had done.

Diondre's hug caught Love by surprise. His six-foot-four frame towered over her when he stood. His height made him look much more like a basketball player than a football player. He had smooth, dark skin that added a defined look to his muscular build. The faint smell of cheap cologne reminded her of how her grandfather smelled when he embraced her. Other than her grandfather, Diondre was the only man that she had had any physical contact with since the passing of her father.

Days later, Diondre and Love became friends. It began with him thanking her in the hallway for helping him study for his exam. Once he found out that he passed his test, he made sure to tell Love the next time that they crossed each other's paths. Diondre found himself becoming attracted to Love and would find a reason every few days to sit in her section of the lunchroom. Each time he asked Love for her assistance, she would gladly do anything she could to help him. His friends and teammates teased him about sitting with Love every lunch hour, but he had already decided that he wanted Love to be his girl. All of his friends liked her and found her to be undeniably beautiful, but they questioned her mental stability since her father died. No one had one bad thing to say about her other than the fact that she was so withdrawn from everyone.

Luckily, Diondre wasn't in this by himself. Love was slowly becoming attracted to him too. He had found a way to gain her trust as a friend and make her smile like she used to. And that's what everyone began to take notice of. At first it was subtle, but soon after, Mrs. Minnie suspected that Love had her eyes fixed on a young man at school. Love used to come home and stay in her room talking on the phone with until she drifted off to sleep. Out of nowhere, Diondre started calling the house every evening at the same time after football practice ended. Soon after, Love was asking Mrs. Minnie if she could go to the football games on Friday nights. Since Mr. Riggs never missed a game, Mrs. Minnie didn't have a problem with her going. She was becoming her old self again.

Shortly thereafter, Love and Diondre became inseparable. Mrs. Minnie was just as happy as her daughter. She was no longer depressed. Her grades were better than they had ever been, and she was beginning to become a social butterfly again. Occasionally, she would visit Whiteville Baptist Church. Her grandparents were so proud of her. They would usually have Sunday dinner at Mrs. Minnie's after church. Sometimes Diondre would join them too.

College scouts from some of the best colleges in the country were coming to the football games to see Diondre play. He was having a season that most high school quarterbacks only dream of. He would have been a much stronger candidate if he could have found a way to do as well in the classroom as he had done on the field. The scouts loved what he could do on the field, but once they saw his grades, they were no longer interested. It didn't take long for him to realize that his dream of playing football at one of the top colleges in the country would no longer come true. He only received offers to play at smaller schools that were not given much recognition during the college football season. He decided that if he could not play at a larger school then he would not play at all. Diondre took it hard, and his father took it even harder. He was extremely disappointed in Diondre, but would never say it.

Mr. Howard would go to work, come home, and watch television until he fell asleep on the couch. He and Diondre never had long conversations about anything. They lived more like roommates than they did as a family. Since Diondre felt forced to stay in Whiteville, his father suggested that he come work at the factory with him when he graduated.

Love's dream was to go to North Carolina Central University and become a lawyer. That dream became much less important when she found out that Diondre wasn't going to college. She tried her best to convince Diondre to attend one of the smaller schools that wanted him, but he didn't change his mind. Right before graduation, he applied for a job at the factory where his father worked. Mr. Howard pushed Diondre's application towards the top of the pile of candidates, and he began working there one week after graduation.

As for Love, she decided to go to attend a local school, Southeastern Community College. Her plan was to study there for two years and then transfer to North Carolina Central University in Durham. She asked Diondre to enroll at Southeastern as well since it was only about eight minutes from both of their homes, but he had given up on college altogether. He figured that he wasn't smart enough, and his father felt the same.

Love didn't have to pay for her education. Mrs. Minnie specifically set aside all of the money from Mr. Harry Lennon's insurance policy to pay for the big events in Love's life and any emergencies that may have come up. She made sure that she never touched that money for any other reason.

Mrs. Minnie bought Love a small car after graduation. Love immediately enrolled into summer classes at Southeastern Community College and was hired as a part-time secretary at Marley Insurance Company.

The workers there had loved her since she was a little girl, and truth be told, she knew more about the insurance business than half of the office because of all those years she shadowed her father.

Love and Diondre spent every free second together. Because of Diondre's popularity, they were invited to all of the parties in Whiteville. Every weekend Mrs. Minnie found herself having to talk to Love about how unladylike it was for her to stay out as late as she did. Diondre would have her out until just before sunrise some mornings. Mrs. Minnie knew that nothing Godly was happening at that time of the night, but she still wanted Love to be able to enjoy her life. Love would listen to Mrs. Minnie for a few weeks, but then revert back to doing the exact opposite of what her mother had told her. Mrs. Minnie would get upset, but could not stay mad at her for long. Love maintained a 4.0 GPA and a job. She was doing well, but her mother still wished that she wouldn't go out and party every weekend.

It was inevitable that Love and Diondre would soon form bad habits. They both started drinking before that summer was over. Surprisingly, Love was the one who influenced Diondre. Love never thought about drinking until they went to a party to help one of her friends celebrate a birthday. All of the birthday girl's closest friends wanted to take a shot of tequila with her. Initially, Love didn't want to, but all of her friends begged her to. When she finally gave in, she insisted that Diondre take a shot with her as well. He agreed. From that moment forward they drank every weekend. Diondre was responsible enough to find a designated driver for them. He vividly remembered watching his drunken mother die in the front seat of the car the night of the accident. He refused to lose Love the same way. Whenever he sent some of Love's friends to pick her up from the house, Mrs. Minnie knew that Love would be drinking that night. She didn't like it, but appreciated the fact that her daughter was smart enough to not drink and drive.

Once Diondre started drinking, his father grew to hate him. He would lecture Diondre about why he shouldn't drink, and even went as far as to threaten a few times that he would kick him out of the house. Diondre quickly grew tired of dealing with his father, and decided that it would be in his best interest to move into a one-bedroom apartment in town. Coincidently, Love soon became frustrated with the talks she and her mother were having, and decided that she would move in with Diondre.

Love broke Mrs. Minnie's heart the day that she moved out. When Love's grandparents found out what had happened, they were devastated. Mr. Riggs didn't take the news as badly as most would have expected. One Saturday morning after he had picked up his daily coffee from the Donut Shop, he stopped by Mrs. Minnie's house. She was just walking out her front door to take her routine walk around the neighborhood when he pulled into the driveway. After all of these years, he still drove that old truck that she drove as a little girl to take the farmhands their lunch. She was relieved that his coming would keep her from leaving. Every now and then she dreaded that walk on Saturday mornings. It wasn't that she didn't enjoy walking, but being an attractive woman caused her to be harassed by a lot of the men in the neighborhood often. Some of them would gawk at her as she walked through. It was the worst on the corner, two blocks away from her house. Those men would drink and sell drugs all day long. When she would walk pass, they wouldn't even try to disguise the fact that they were staring. Although they never said anything disrespectful, they still made her uncomfortable.

Mr. Riggs began speaking as soon as they sat down on the front porch.

"Minnie, she's not a little girl anymore you know. You have to let her grow up the only way she's going to grow up-that's by living her life." Mrs. Minnie had no idea that he would start talking about Love. She sat back in her chair and awaited the next thing her father would say as he paused to take a sip of his coffee.

"Your mom and I did it. You and Harry did the same thing. You just gotta' suck it up and let her grow up. Everybody's gotta' live their own lives, baby. Now you know how I felt when you popped up shacking with Harry. Karma's a nasty slut ain't it?" He tilted his head over and looked at her out of the corner of his eye with a slight grin. That lightened the mood, and also gave Mrs. Minnie a little comfort. She still didn't like it, but in that moment she learned that the only thing that she could do is accept it.

Love and Diondre felt liberated together. Drinking on the weekends quickly turned into a daily habit for Diondre. As soon as he came in from work each day, his first stop would be to the refrigerator to grab a beer to help him unwind. He would be drunk before Love came home from work. Soon, she picked up the same habit. Her poison of choice was cheap wine from the grocery store. She would savor the taste right out the bottle while she did her homework until it was all gone.

That liberation they felt (the liberation that almost every young person feels when they move away from home for the first time) proved to be too much too soon for their young minds. After drinking,

57

they started smoking weed. First Diondre, and then Love. All of their friends were doing it, so quite naturally it was their next step.

Cocaine slowly became the drug of choice on the party scene around that time. There seemed to be more and more young people sniffing that white powder in every club and at every party. On Diondre's nineteenth birthday, Love threw him a surprise party in their apartment. It was a small group of their closest friends. The alcohol fueled night resulted in the police having to come by to give them a warning about their music being too loud. It was by God's grace they didn't come inside and ask to see any of their I.D's. Everyone in that apartment would have been taken to jail. Unfortunately, the night ended with Love and Diondre trying cocaine for the first time. That night began a long journey that they would both grow to regret.

Everyone noticed that Love had become a different person. She was showing up late for work at Marley's Insurance each day. Her grades were also dropping. When Mrs. Minnie would see her and Diondre, usually on

Sunday evenings when the family would get together for dinner, she could clearly see that they were traveling on the wrong path. Every mother can sense when their children aren't doing well.

To make matters worse, Love's menstrual cycle didn't come one month. Initially, she didn't think too much of it because it happened to her before when she was around sixteen. But when she didn't have it the very next month, she knew that she was pregnant. Diondre was excited when she broke the news to him. Her co-workers and friends were happy and congratulated her when she told them. Mrs. Minnie, on the other hand, didn't take it too well. She knew that a child meant that Love would probably not be transferring to North Carolina Central University as planned, or any other four-year institution for that matter. But truthfully, even she and Mr. Harry Lennon conceived Love out of wedlock. History was repeating itself.

During Love's pregnancy, she stopped drinking, but couldn't seem to stop using cocaine. Diondre still drank more often and used all sorts of drugs. However, he had no idea that the mother of his future child was still using. Mrs. Minnie would go with Love to her doctor visits when Diondre wasn't able to get off of work. After Love was given the results of her routine prenatal check up, Mrs. Minnie discovered that Love was using cocaine. She knew that Love had been drinking before her pregnancy, but would have never thought that her daughter was using cocaine.

Mrs. Minnie loved Love more than life itself, but she was not going to allow Love to destroy the life that she had growing inside of her. She called Mr. Riggs, Diondre, and Mr. Harry Lennon's parents so that they could sit Love down for an intervention at her home. Diondre was extremely upset because he had no idea that Love was still using cocaine while she was carrying his child. His anger forced him to confess about all of the drinking and drugs they had been using. After everyone had spoken, Mrs. Minnie presented Love with the idea of participating in a sixty-day rehab program in Raleigh. She offered to pay the cost for Love and Diondre if they agreed to take the program seriously. Diondre refused. He didn't feel as though his problem was that serious. Love took her mother's offer in an effort to save her and her child's lives.

A week later she packed her bags and checked into the Life Again Drug Treatment Facility in Raleigh. No one said a word to anyone. She told the owner of Marley Insurance that she would need to take a break from there until she had the baby. When people asked Love's family where she had been, they told them that she was living with one of Mrs. Minnie's family members who was a nurse in Smithfield due to pregnancy complications that required her to be closely monitored.

The rehabilitation clinic worked wonders for Love. She finished the rest of her pregnancy drug-free, and delivered a healthy baby boy named Bryce Lennon. Diondre and Love agreed that the baby shouldn't carry his last name because they weren't married yet. Just as Mr. Riggs and Mr. Harry Lennon's parents spoiled Love when she was born, they spoiled Bryce. They wouldn't let him out their sight.

A few weeks after Bryce was born, Love had started back working at Marley Insurance and continued classes at Southeastern. Everything was going well for Diondre and Love for a while. Bryce would spend a few days a week in daycare and the other days with Mr. Harry Lennon's parents. Most weekends, Mrs. Minnie would offer to keep Bryce. She knew that Love and Diondre needed a break. With freedom from parenting on the weekends, Love and Diondre eventually started drinking and using drugs as much as they had done not too long before.

Love was once again late for work on a regular basis, and her grades began to deteriorate. She tried using Bryce as an excuse, but Marley Insurance was left with no choice but to let her go. She had also missed far too many days of classes to make up her work. Meanwhile, Diondre's job performance at work was horrible. Showing up late became normal for him. His father tried to warn him that he was in jeopardy of losing his job, but the talk proved to come too late. The following day after their conversation, he came in late to work and was fired as soon as he walked in.

The more time Love and Diondre spent feeding their habits, the more time Bryce was forced to spend with his grandmother. Diondre's unemployment checks were barely enough to pay the few bills of the house. Love quickly found a job as a waitress at a restaurant that was known to have the best soul food in the area, Nana's. People would drive from as far as twenty miles away to eat there. Love had to work much harder there than she had to at Marley's Insurance, but was content because the pay was better.

On Sunday afternoons, the members of Whiteville Baptist Church would come eat dinner at Nana's and graciously tip Love. Sometimes she would leave that restaurant with over two-hundred dollars in tip money alone. Love was excellent at her job. She was just as personable as her father, and was by far one of the most beautiful women in the county. Everyone that came in that restaurant adored her just as much as they had when she was a young girl. However, they were unaware that the more money she made, the more she and Diondre splurged on cocaine.

Nana's was a good job for as long as it lasted, but Love's habits always seemed to get in the way of anything positive in her life. Right before she found out that she was pregnant for the second time, Love got herself fired. Diondre worked whenever he could find someone that was willing to pay him. Love made money cleaning homes in the area.

News of her second pregnancy was not a surprise to Love's family. They knew that it would only be a matter of time before she would carry another child. Although she didn't use as much cocaine this pregnancy as she did with her last one, she still used enough to risk the healthy delivery of her child. Many people prayed for her and the baby. Thankfully, God answered them and blessed Love with a little girl named Alexia Lennon.

Bryce had just turned three-years-old when Alexia was born. Alexia's smile encouraged Love to try a drug rehabilitation clinic one more time. However, she didn't make it halfway through the program before she was back home snorting cocaine again.

The viscous crack epidemic swept throughout the United States a few years after Alexia was born, and Love and Diondre were caught in the middle of it. Bryce and Alexia were spending most of their time with Mrs. Minnie. After Mrs. Minnie would get off work, she would pick them up from the daycare and watch them until the next morning when Mr. Riggs would pick them up from the house and take them back to daycare. Diondre and Love were too strung out on drugs to be responsible parents.

Life had become very hard for the young parents. Neither one of them could keep a job for longer than three months at a time. They owed money to almost everyone they knew and were constantly having to move from one apartment to another because they were always too far behind on their rent. It wasn't long before Diondre began stealing to support their habits. Within a few years, he had been charged with multiple petty theft crimes, but would never spend more than a few months in jail.

Love somehow managed to remain beautiful in spite of her hard living. With the lifestyle that she chose to live, that was both a blessing and a curse. For years, all of the drug dealers that she bought drugs from attempted to sleep with her. She would flirt and tease them without giving them the satisfaction of being physically intimate with her. But once she became completely addicted and could no longer afford her habit, she gave in to their fantasies. At first, she was selective and private about her ordeals and would only sleep with a few of the dealers around town. However, the moment soon came when she no longer cared and did whatever she had to with whomever she had to in order to satisfy her addiction. Diondre was well aware of what she did and encouraged her to do so any time they had run out of money. Getting high was the only thing he was in love with at that point.

Throughout those years, they always hoped that they would get off of the streets. Diondre would enroll into a rehabilitation program at the end of each short jail stay.

He tried really hard to kick his long time habit. Not too long after, Love would be inspired to join a program as well. But by that time, Diondre would already be using again. When one of them was in the program the other would always be consumed with living recklessly.¬¬¬ It seemed as though they could never get their lives back on track at the same time.

Mrs. Minnie, Mr. Riggs, and Mr. Harry Lennon's parents completely gave up on Love as did Mr. Howard with Diondre. They loved them both, but at this point in their lives there was nothing left to do but pray that God would protect them.

Eight years after Alexia's birth, Love gave birth to a beautiful boy, Deon Lennon. Love had no doubt in her mind that Diondre was Deon's father, but Diondre was skeptical because Love had been having sex with multiple men in exchange for cocaine. Although that thought was strong in his heart, his pride wouldn't let him take a paternity test. Love suggested that he get one so that he could have a clear mind, but he still refused.

After Deon was born, Love and Diondre decided that their children should live with Mrs. Minnie to give them time to better themselves. Love moved to the projects and Diondre bounced around between any friends or family members that would give him a room. Love made sure that she visited her children every Sunday. She was making progress, but the process was slow.

Mrs. Minnie developed a deep anger in her heart for Diondre and blamed him for the irresponsible woman Love had become. She felt like he was the cause of Love's turn for the worst. She believed if she would have been a little stricter with her daughter when she was younger, she could have saved Love from a world of hurt. Mrs. Minnie would only allow Diondre to see the children every other weekend at her house. He could not leave the house with them without her accompanying him. The entire time that he was there she would look at him with a slightly evil look on her face. Most of the times that Diondre was supposed to visit, he would not come, leaving Mrs. Minnie with the chore of explaining to his children why he didn't love them like their mother did.

Mrs. Minnie had her hands full trying to raise those kids. She loved them more than herself, but taking care of all three of them became hectic. She ended up retiring early from the school system so that she could stay home and raise them. They loved their grandmother more than anyone else in the world. At ages nineteen, sixteen, and eight, Love's children grew to accept their reality and love those things that were pleasant in it. They were taught at an early age that in order to truly love anything, they must be equally willing to be hurt by it.

# Chapter 2. All Things Beautiful Eventually Die

As Deon ran up the stairs on that morning to wake Bryce and Alexia, he thought about what Mrs. Minnie had told him about God not getting mad enough to kill anyone. He was eager for a better understanding, but was content at the moment with knowing that God wasn't going to kill him. When he got to the top of the stairs, Alexia was storming out of Bryce's room frustrated, as usual. It seemed like she was always frustrated with him in the mornings. She was definitely not a morning person.

"I wish you would get your crap together! I'm tired of this mess now!" Alexia screamed back at Bryce as she walked across the hallway into the bathroom and slammed the door. She was too upset to notice her little brother standing at the top of the stairs.

Alexia was the spitting image of her mother when she was her age. They had the same brunette hair, slender physique, and naturally tanned complexion. The difference was Alexia's faint freckles. She was a straight-

70

A student, cheerleader, and member of the Beta Club, who was loved by all of her teachers and classmates. But she had a horrible attitude at times. She was a sweet girl until someone pissed her off. And Bryce always found a way to piss her off.

Alexia aided Bryce with his Art business. Because he had not been checking his business email account like he should, he had no idea that five individuals were interested in doing business with him. Alexia was highly upset with him. She admired his work, but wished he would be a little more responsible when it came to his business. It was one of the busiest times of the year for him with Valentine's Day quickly approaching.

Bryce was a talented young artist who had been interested in painting and drawing since he was a small child. He won many awards throughout the years for his paintings. His first noteworthy assignment was to paint a family portrait on a large canvas for the mayor. The mayor's daughter was in Bryce's ninth grade class and wanted to give her parents something that they could cherish as a wedding anniversary present. The mayor was so impressed with his work that he placed it in the main hallway of the City Hall office. Everyone who came into that building was mesmerized when they saw it. Before long, the editor of the local newspaper had written an article about his work and then he began receiving phone calls from people all over the county who were interested in purchasing portraits from him. In between assignments, he would set up a booth at the flea market on the weekends and draw sketches of people who sat at his table. Being this committed to his craft developed him into a flawless artist at a very young age. He was skilled beyond his years and worked incredibly fast. Once he put up his website, Alexia helped him with marketing and his business began to thrive.

Alexia made sure that everyone knew who her brother was and handled most of the administrative work of his business. The only problem was, like most siblings, they argued about the smallest things all of the time. If Bryce didn't follow-up with people that were emailing him, Alexia would yell at him. If he was behind schedule with a painting, Alexia would yell at him. She didn't care that it took time for the creative process to develop. All she cared about was sending invoices and receiving payments. She could not do her job effectively if Bryce didn't do his and that always made her upset.

Deon screamed out from the top of the stairs "Grandma said come on. It's time to eat," and hurried back down to the kitchen. Mrs. Minnie had already set the table and was sitting down waiting on them to come downstairs. The smell of all the food made Deon's mouth water as soon as he walked into the kitchen. There was sweet apple bacon, scrambled eggs, Pender smoked sausage, toast, and Deon's favorite-cheese grits.

Bryce came down first with a canvas of his in the leather carrying case he used to make personal deliveries and sat down at the head of the table. He preferred to deliver his work in person over shipping it in the mail so that he could see his customers' first reactions to his work.

Bryce was a freshman at Southeastern Community College. He had been a barely average student throughout school and his business was doing well so he opted to wait a year after graduating high school before enrolling into college. He was more like his father than Deon and Alexia. He was tall and built like him and had inherited his dark skin, but had never been interested in playing any sports. His passion for art kept him occupied. Deon was Bryce's biggest fan. He would watch him paint for hours and always be amazed at the end result.

Alexia was always last to come down. She was a prima donna in her own right. She would spend the whole morning in the bathroom and come downstairs with a simple pair of jeans and a nice blouse. Her perfectly-parted straight hair and beautifully applied make-up made her look like a Barbie.

"Did you respond to those emails?" Alexia asked as she made her way into the kitchen and sat down at the table.

"No, girl! I was going to get to all of them today when I dropped off this order, but you ain't giving me time to!" Before Alexia could respond, like she always defensively did when she and Bryce got into it, Mrs. Minnie interrupted.

"Now y'all know y'all not going to talk about no business at this table this early in the morning. And y'all definitely not going to be arguing. Not today! No!" Mrs. Minnie extended her hands to Alexia and Deon and they all bowed their heads in prayer. Mrs. Minnie had the same routine almost every morning after breakfast. She would take Bryce to the post office to ship out any orders he had that were too far away to hand deliver, drop him off at school, and then come home to home-school Deon. Alexia would usually catch a ride with one of her friends who drove to school.

When everyone was almost finished eating that morning, Mrs. Minnie asked Bryce if she could take a look at the painting. When he pulled it out, Mrs. Minnie stared at it perplexedly.

"What in the Heavens is that?!? Lord Jesus the whole world is going crazy."

It was Lisa Taylor's order. It was the first of its kind for Bryce. It was a portrait of a broken heart split into two equal halves. The left half was the side view of a very attractive young woman who wore a black dress. Her eyes were closed, and her lips were puckered as if she was kissing someone. The right half displayed a handsome young man dressed in a black suit, white shirt, and black bowtie. He was facing the woman with his lips puckered as if he was about to kiss her. The caption at the top of the canvas read '*It's Over.*' After catching him cheating on her more than once, Lisa Taylor decided to end her relationship with her boyfriend on Valentine's Day. The painting had such great detail and brilliant colors. Bryce's work was nothing short of genius.

"So that's why you haven't been taking care of your business?!?! You were on the phone with that chick all week long, and last week, and working on that one dang painting!" she asserted as she got up from the table and made her way back upstairs.

Alexia was no fool. She remembered when Lisa Taylor's emails came through their website. Lisa sent a photo and a description of what she wanted, as every costumer had to do when they inquired about pricing. Alexia was against Bryce doing it from the beginning. Normally, he would have charged one hundred-fifty dollars for an assignment like that, but after seeing how attractive she was, he sent her a quote for ninety dollars. Alexia was floored when she saw the quote in their sent box.

Bryce and Lisa talked all week long on the phone while he worked on that painting. Rarely were any of the conversations about business. Alexia sensed that Lisa was pretending to be attracted to Bryce in order to get her painting at a cheaper rate, and it upset her. She owned twenty percent of the business and wanted to make sure that she was paid every penny she deserved for the work she did. The two of them worked hard enough to never have to ask Mrs. Minnie for anything.

Mrs. Minnie left with the children so that they could be dropped off at school. Bryce wouldn't need for Mrs. Minnie to pick him up that day because he was going to hand deliver Lisa Taylor's painting. She lived in a small town named Clarkton, which was located in the neighboring county. But she and a few of her friends booked a hotel room in Whiteville on Valentine's Day weekend so that they could celebrate her upcoming breakup.

After dropping Bryce off, Mrs. Minnie and Deon returned home to begin their usual routine of cleaning the house before they began working on the school lessons for that day. Mrs. Minnie heard the house phone ringing as soon as she and Deon reached the front porch. When she made it inside to the kitchen and answered the phone, all she could hear was coughing. She immediately knew that it was Love.

"Baby, me and Deon just walked in the house. Let me get settled and I'm going to call you back in a few okay?"

Love just hung up the phone. She was coughing too hard to respond right away. Deon had already started clearing the table and putting the dishes into the dishwasher by the time Mrs. Minnie hung up the phone.

"That was my mama wasn't it?"

"Yea, I have to call her back. Now let's hurry up and get this house cleaned up. Someone has a math test today at eleven o'clock right after we do some English."

"I'm ready for the math test, but do we really have to do English today, Grandma?"

"Yes you have to do English. Matter of fact, the next time you say that about my favorite subject, we're going to do English all day long for a week," she sarcastically said as she walked out of the kitchen to go to her room to call Love back.

"I want to talk to Mama when you get finished, Grandma."

"Go ahead and vacuum the living room after you get all the dishes finished, baby. I'll give you the phone right after then."

Mrs. Minnie rested on her bed and called her daughter. Love had seen plenty of doctors over the past few months. At first she thought the coughing was due to a cold, but she never got any better. She had lost a lot of weight, but confessed that she had not been using as much as she had in the past. She told her mother that she was trying really hard to quit. Love would even come to church a couple of Sundays each month.

"Hey Mama," she said, trying her best to control the cough.

"Hey Love. Did they give you something for your cough today? It sounds like it's getting worse every time we talk, baby." Mrs. Minnie didn't like hearing Love suffer.

There was a short moment of silence after Mrs. Minnie spoke. In that moment Love could hear the sound of the vacuum cleaner in the background. She knew it was Deon and that made her smile as she sat down on the worn couch in the living room of her apartment. Mrs. Minnie could hear Love smoking in between those horrible coughs.

"Mama, the test results got back today…" Love began crying before she could continue. Mrs. Minnie quickly sat up in her bed.

"Talk to me, baby. What did they say?"

"Ma, I have stage IV ovarian cancer."

Mrs. Minnie couldn't hear everything that Love said because of her crying, but was in denial that she had heard the word cancer.

"Love, what did you say, baby? I can't make out what you're saying."

"Stage IV ovarian cancer, Mama."

Mrs. Minnie heard her clearly that time. The tears immediately started rolling down her cheek, but she made sure that Love didn't hear her crying. Mrs. Minnie was as strong as she could be and stayed on the phone to comfort Love as she cried.

"It's going to be okay, Love. God is in control. It's going to be okay."

81

Mr. Riggs stopped by the house to check on the family around this time. Mrs. Minnie could hear him and Deon talking in the front of the house. As she was attempting to keep her composure, Deon ran into the room.

"Grandma, let me talk to Mama."

"Not right now sweetie. I'll come get you when I'm finished talking to her."

When Love heard Deon's voice she quickly asked her mother if she could speak to him. Mrs. Minnie knew that this was not the best time for Love to talk to her son, but she gave him the phone anyway.

"Here she is. I'm going to go in there and talk to Grandpa."

Mrs. Minnie left the bedroom and walked into the living room where Mr. Riggs was watching television and drinking his morning cup of coffee. He knew something was bothering her as soon as she walked into the room. When she was sure that Deon could no longer hear her, she began to cry.

"What's wrong, Minnie?"

Mrs. Minnie motioned for her father to follow her outside to the porch. As soon as he closed the door behind him, he was met with the sight of his daughter crying profusely as she sat down on the cushioned porch bench.

Mr. Riggs sat down beside her, and embraced her. He could only hope that he would be able to say something to her to comfort her whenever she decided to tell him what had happened.

"It's Love, Daddy. She just got her test results back today and they're saying she has stage IV cancer."

"Dear God." Mr. Riggs closed his eyes and slowly leaned back on the bench. It was devastating news that neither of them was prepared for.

"Daddy, I knew something was wrong. Love hasn't been to the doctor in years and that cough. It just kept getting worse and worse. My baby..." She was trying not to fall apart completely, but she couldn't stop the tears from flowing. Mr. Riggs held her tight. He would be there for as long as she needed him to be.

Suddenly, Deon came running out of the front door to give the cordless phone to his grandmother. As soon as they saw him, they tried to change the looks on their faces.

"Mama said that she's going to call back later on tonight, Grandma. She said she's real sick and needs to talk to all of us about something, I don't know…Grandma, you've been crying?"

"No, baby. My sinuses started bothering me as soon as we came outside. What did you and your mama talk about?"

"Nothing much. She told me that she was sick and was coughing the whole time we was on the phone. She's had that cold for a looong time. I told her to take something. Then she told me that she was going to call back later on and hung up. I'm gon' go get ready for my math test. Y'all can stay out here as long as you want." Deon slipped back into the house hoping they stayed out there and talked so he wouldn't have to do any English assignments.

Mr. Riggs had to drive to Smithfield later that day to meet with his business partners about the tobacco farms. He wanted to visit Love and check on her before he left town, but he figured that she needed more time to cope with the news she had just been given. Mrs. Minnie didn't give Deon an English lesson that day. She gave him his math test early, and went into her room so that she could pray for her daughter and for direction.

Once Alexia got out of school that day, she decided to ride the bus instead of catching a ride with one of her friends. She loved riding with them, but on Fridays they always wanted to ride through town and spend time with each other. It would be hours before she could get home. Alexia was extremely tired, and just wanted to get home to take a nap.

The projects were on the bus route she took to get home. There were about ten of her schoolmates that were dropped off there. Those projects were just like any other housing project that you can imagine. There were always people who sat outside in small groups in front of their apartments to pass the time. Some worked hard to get out of the projects hoping to soon see a better day while others were content with doing whatever they could just to get by. Everyone in the projects coped with the poverty that plagued the town in his or her own way. Some chose drugs and alcohol while others simply gave up and dealt with life's problems as they arose. In spite of the way they lived, the one thing that was evident was that they all loved each other. The soul of that community was stronger than most communities around the world. However, people who lived outside of this area chose to focus more on the living conditions of the community than they did the people who were living there.

As Alexia was staring out of the window when the bus stopped in the projects that day, she saw her mother walking out of her apartment. She had looked much smaller than Alexia had ever remembered seeing her. Her hair was unkempt and she wore a yellow sundress and an old acid washed jacket that were both entirely too big for her frame. The sun didn't make her skin glow like it used to. It was more than obvious that the natural tan that once gave her an exotic appeal had turned pale. Still, she was beautiful. She was coughing horribly as she walked towards the bus.

Alexia slowly slumped down in her seat after she noticed her mother and pretended to have fallen asleep. She could hear some of the children on the bus snickering behind her. One was even bold enough to intentionally whisper "crackhead" loud enough so that others around would hear. Alexia paid them no attention. Those few immature kids had picked on Alexia behind her back for years because her mother was on drugs.

Over the years, Alexia grew to hate her mother. She had often heard growing up that she was just like her mother, but Alexia could not see beyond the drug using prostitute that she had grown to be. It disgusted her to know that Love gave away her children just so that she could keep living the way she had for so many years. She believed her mother loved her, but loved the drugs and alcohol more than she loved her or any of her siblings. As the bus pulled away, she wished that she would have stayed with her friends until they drove her home. She hated riding that bus because she knew there was always a possibility that she would see her mother. That ended up being one of the longest rides home in her life.

As for Bryce, he only had three classes that day and his day dragged along. He spent his break in the forever loud and crowded student lounge as he had always done. Usually, Bryce wouldn't show his work to anyone before the customer had seen it, but he was so proud of this painting that he showed it off to a small group of friends as soon as they asked to see it. They were impressed with his work. It was different, and the fact that a woman would give it to her boyfriend as a way to end their relationship on Valentine's Day made it that much more interesting. Lisa Taylor was the one of the sexiest women that most of those guys had ever seen. His friends believed that he exaggerated how she looked in the painting. They couldn't believe a woman that beautiful lived so close them and they hadn't seen her or heard about her. Bryce didn't argue with them. He showed them the original picture she sent him on his phone. They were absolutely shocked.

Bryce and Lisa sent text messages to each other throughout the day. She was excited about finally getting the chance to meet the artist behind her painting. Bryce had arranged for him to get a ride to the hotel after school and was anxious to meet her.

When class was dismissed, he hopped in the car with his classmate and headed straight there. When he called and let her know that he was on the way, he could hear her two friends and loud music in the background. He could tell that they had already started celebrating Lisa's breakup weekend. As soon as he got to the hotel, he called again to let her know that he was there.

"Come on down to the end of the right side of the building. I'm in the very last room. My girls are going to step out for a while. They should be passing you in the parking lot. But anyway, come on down.

I'm so excited!!!" Bryce could tell that she was just as anxious as he was, and her high-pitched voice was a sweet sound to his ears.

As he walked down the side of the building, he heard loud music coming from the car that was approaching. There were two beautiful young ladies inside dancing and singing as if they had not one care in the world. He figured that they must have been Lisa's friends. It made sense that she would have friends who were just as beautiful as she was.

Once he made it inside the hotel, he instantly became nervous. He had no time to gather himself. He was almost to her room. He stopped and took a few deep breaths before he crossed the doorway that was about three rooms down from hers. No sooner than he had begun walking again he heard a door open. There she was. And he was stunned speechless. The pictures that he had seen of her did not do her justice. She had beautiful, long, straight hair with the most inviting smile Bryce had ever seen. She wore a white maxi-dress that fit every curve of her athletic build. The sun's rays made it apparent that there was not one blemish on her swarthy skin. She was taller than he expected, maybe five-foot seven. Ms. Lisa Taylor was absolutely gorgeous.

"Bryce, you couldn't get here fast enough," she said as she greeted him with a hug.

"Come on in, I've been waiting on it all week. You got to excuse the mess in here. Those girls are hell on hotel rooms."

"Don't worry about it. I'm sure my room is a whole lot messier."

When he walked in behind her, he noticed a huge bottle of vodka on the table that sat in front of the window. There was a container of cranberry juice beside it, and an open empty pizza box with cigar guts in it. The room smelled like he was standing right in the middle of a burning marijuana field. It was evident that Lisa had already started drinking. Bryce could smell the alcohol on her when she hugged him. From the look of the bottle, she and her friends had drunk a lot in the short period of time they had been there.

Lisa sat down on the bed anxiously waiting on Bryce to show her the painting. He carefully pulled it out and placed it on the bed beside her. She couldn't believe what was placed in front of her. She was completely amazed!

"It's beautiful Bryce!! I knew it was going to come out good when you started, but I had no idea...I have something for you."

Lisa got up from the bed and walked over to the counter beside the sink at the far end of the room. Bryce sat down on the bed and reexamined the painting's fine details once more. He was pleased with his work and could tell just how quickly his skills were developing. When he looked up, she was reaching into her pocketbook so that she could pay him.

"I know we talked about ninety dollars, but I was able to do a little more. I really appreciate it Bryce." Lisa handed Bryce one hundred-fifty dollars. Giving her the discount worked itself out.

"So, do you drink?" she softly asked as she walked over to the vodka on the table. Bryce could tell that she was a little tipsy. Her speech wasn't slurred, but she had been having a tough time keeping her balance since he got there.

"Not really…"

"Just have one with me please. Relax Bryce. Enjoy yourself. I know you don't just go to school and do all of that painting without having any fun. Just one."

The truth was the only time Bryce had ever taken a drink was when he and one of his friends snuck into the kitchen and got into the communion wine at his great grandparent's church during Vacation Bible School a few years ago. But here he was in this hotel room with the beautiful Ms. Lisa Taylor asking him to take just one with her.

"I guess one wouldn't hurt. But after this one, that's it."

Lisa grabbed two cups, poured the liquor on hard and added a little cranberry for color. Bryce had no idea how much liquor she had put in that cup. He had never had it before. Lisa sat down on the other bed across from him and they talked. She giggled at the fact that Bryce was having a drink only to impress her. As fast as he was drinking, it would only be a matter of time before he felt the effects.

The more Bryce drank, the sexier Lisa looked. As she sat there telling him all of the details of her boyfriend cheating, he gazed in her eyes. Bryce chose not to say anything. He figured that she really needed to vent. She, on the other hand, knew that he was deeply attracted to her and would do anything to please her. Every few moments the thought of it made her blush.

About an hour into his stay, Lisa's two friends had come back. They were talking a million miles a minute and laughing loudly when they opened the door. As soon as they realized that Bryce was there, they lowered their voices and ran over to see the painting.

"O-M-G! This is amazing! I'm Antoinette. I'm Lisa's best friend, and this is Brittany, her other best friend," Antoinette said. Brittany stood beside Antoinette admiring the painting.

"It's a pleasure to meet you, ladies. I'm Bryce."

"I bet that bastard won't cheat on nobody else when he see this!" Brittany said as she high-fived Antoinette.

"Ooooh Lisa we got it girl! I was in there talking and Brittany caught him slipping good," Antoinette said.

Brittany reached into her large designer purse and pulled out a sandwich bag full of pills and another small plastic bag of weed. Lisa jumped up from the bed and quickly grabbed the bag of colorful pills.

"How in the hell did y'all get all of these!?!? He's going to kill us!" Lisa screamed.

"He ain't going to kill nobody girl. He's not even going to miss it. That boy had hundreds of them in there. We only got a couple. Where are those cigars we had?" Brittany asked.

Bryce had never seen anything like it. He did everything he could to stay away from drugs because of what they did to his mother and father. There had to be over forty pills in that bag. Before he could ask what kind of pills they were, Lisa had popped two in her mouth. Antoinette found the cigars and rolled up some of the weed from the other bag. Brittany poured herself a drink and turned the television to the channel that played the top 40 R&B hits. It all happened so fast. Bryce knew in his heart that it was time for him to leave. He sat there for a second, and then decided that he had to know what those girls were getting themselves into.

"I don't mean to be nosey, but what kind of pills are those?"

"That's 'X' Bryce. You know, ecstasy. Wait a minute. You mean to tell me that you've never seen anybody take ecstasy before?" Antoinette said as she reached in the bag.

When he stood up to leave, Lisa stood right up with him and attempted to convince him to stay.

"Bryce, you just got here. Don't tell me you're going to get all weird and try to leave me hanging?"

"I was just going to go use the bathroom, if you don't mind." He was trying to stay calm, but truthfully he was just as nervous as he was when he first got there. The only reason he even contemplated staying was because he could tell that Lisa was really into him. He had girlfriends before, but none of them were as attractive as she was.

When he was in the bathroom all he could think about was what she was planning to do with the portrait. After he came back into the bedroom, he asked her.

"Lisa, how are you going to give that painting to your boyfriend?"

All of them laughed hysterically at his question. Bryce managed to smile, but he was really interested in knowing.

"I'm going to have it delivered to him. I know his nosey mom and even nosier sister will be right there to watch him open it when it comes to his house. Every one of them has lied to me trying to cover up his dirt, so I hope they're all there when he opens it."

Lisa seemed to get angrier with each second that passed. She was a woman scorned indeed. Bryce couldn't understand why anybody would spend that much money to break up with someone, but he figured that people had probably done crazier things.

Bryce sat down on the bed next to Lisa, while Antoinette and Brittany sat across from them on the other. Those girls drank vodka, smoked weed, gossiped, and giggled for what seemed like an eternity. Bryce never did have another drink. He was actually enjoying the chance to become more acquainted with Lisa. As time passed, Lisa became more physical with Bryce. She wanted to touch him and lay on him. Bryce knew that it was the ecstasy.

Both Antoinette and Brittany had been texting on their cell phones trying to figure out what they would be doing later on that evening. Lisa didn't want to go anywhere, but they didn't care. Those girls were ready to party for the entire weekend.

By nightfall, he knew that it was time for him to leave. He couldn't go home that night though. Mrs. Minnie would be extremely upset if he came into her house with the scent of marijuana and alcohol on his clothes. He would have to spend the night with Mr. Riggs. Luckily, he lived only a few blocks up the street. He said his goodbyes to Antoinette and Brittany, and walked outside with Lisa. Once the door closed behind them, Bryce had turned to hug her goodbye, but was met with an erotic, passionate kiss.

Bryce walked to Mr. Riggs' home with the biggest smile plastered across his face as he thought of the wild and crazy time he had just had with those girls. He was ecstatic, and had every reason to be. He made more money than he expected on the painting and one of the sexiest girls he had ever seen in his life was all over him. It had been a great night.

When he arrived at Mr. Riggs' home there wasn't any sign of life there. The truck was gone and all of the lights inside of the house were off. Bryce had an extra key to the house, but he was a little concerned. Mr. Riggs was usually at home that time of night. He fumbled through his keys to find the right one. That one cup of vodka was enough to make even the simplest tasks difficult. Once he got inside, he headed for the refrigerator to get him some water. All of that alcohol had made him extremely thirsty. He drank almost a gallon of water straight out the jug.

After he finished, he called Mr. Riggs to see where he was so he could let him know that he was there. Bryce walked in the spacious living room, turned the fan on, and flopped down on the couch after Mr. Riggs didn't answer. As he stared at the ceiling in that dark room, all he could do was think about Lisa. A few minutes later, his thoughts were interrupted by the ringing of his phone. It was his grandfather.

"Sorry I missed your call Bryce. That prune juice from earlier just kicked in a little while ago…"

"That's too much information, sir. I was in your neck of the woods, and decided to spend the night over here at your house. I just got here. Where are you?"

"I had some business to take care of up here in Smithfield and decided to just spend the night. Hey, there's plenty of food in the fridge and you know where everything is. I'm 'bout to turn in Bryce. I'm tired as a dog. Just lock up when you leave, alright?"

"Okay. I'm about to do the same thing. I'll give you a call in the morning when I head home. Get some sleep."

He must have stared at that ceiling for thirty minutes trying to fall asleep. All he could do was think about Lisa. He wanted to call her or text her, but he did not want to bother her. He thought that it would be best for her to enjoy her friends this weekend. He would call her another time. Shortly after, he fell asleep.

All of that water he drank woke him up and sent him racing down the hallway to the bathroom in the middle of the night. When he returned to the couch and checked his cell phone, he noticed that he had received a few text messages while he was asleep. To his surprise they were all from Lisa.

10:39 P.M. -I MISS YOU LIKE CRAZY ALREADY! I DON'T THINK I'M GOING OUT WITH THEM

11:08 P.M. -THEY'RE GONE AND I'M WIDE AWAKE FEELING GOOD. ARE YOU
CLOSE BY??? CALL ME
11:17 P.M. -I WANT TO SEE YOU IF YOU'RE AROUND

Bryce couldn't do anything but smile as he read them. He called her immediately. After all, it had only been about twenty minutes since her last message. Lisa picked up the phone on the first ring.

"Hey, where are you?"

"I'm right up the street. I thought you'd be partied out by now. Y'all were going hard when I was there."

He could almost hear her blush through the phone. She wasn't trying to hide the fact that she was into him.

"Come back to the hotel. I'm here all by myself. They tried to drag me out with them, but I don't feel like dealing with all that tonight. I texted you a million times. I thought you were ignoring me."

"I'll be there in about thirty minutes. Let me get myself together."

As soon as Bryce got off the phone, he decided he needed to take a shower before he left. It was almost midnight when he started walking back to the hotel. The night was young for a lot of people that evening. Music from the car stereos filled the air and the occasional horn honking from random cars as he walked made him feel energized. The short nap he took at Mr. Riggs' house had worked wonders for him. The vodka had almost worn off completely.

When he arrived in front of Lisa's room and knocked on the door, he could hear the soft sound of love music coming from inside. When she opened the door, the scent of marijuana was stronger than it had been earlier. Lisa smoked so much that her eyes were nearly closed shut. She had changed into a simple tank top and shorts from the white-fitting maxi dress that she had on earlier.

Bryce saw that the vodka bottle was more than half empty. They must have drunk for hours after he left.

"So, don't I get a hug, Bryce?" she seductively asked as soon as he sat down on the bed.

He turned to hug her, but she quickly turned that moment into yet another passionate kiss. This one wasn't as aggressive as the goodbye kiss from earlier, but it was intense. As the music played from the television, she embraced him even tighter. Bryce could taste the smoke and alcohol that lingered in her mouth. After a minute of kissing, it was clear that Lisa wanted more. Bryce kindly unlocked his lips from hers and took a seat on the bed, but she continued to pursue him. In that moment, he knew what was about to happen.

"You must have taken some more of those 'X' pills."

"Uh-huh. I took another one right after we got off the phone." She became more erotic with every passing minute. Bryce had only been with one woman in his lifetime, but at this point, he was sure that he and Lisa were about to take their friendship to the next level. And once their passions could no longer be held back, it happened.

At the end of their episode, Bryce rolled over from on top of her and happily gazed at the ceiling. He looked over at her as she lay there completely still. It was hard to see her in the dark. The television was still on, but had gone black during their moment of passion. He got out of the bed to wash up in the bathroom. When he finished, he noticed that Lisa had not moved an inch or made a sound. He called her name, but she did not respond. He shook her shoulder as he sat down on the bed. She was still laying there lifeless and her skin was much hotter than it should have been. Bryce panicked. He kept shaking her, but she wouldn't wake up. He was left with no choice but to make an emergency call.

"911 dispatch. What's your emergency?"

"Hey. I'm at the Best Western hotel and my friend…She isn't moving or responding to anything. I think she took some pills." Bryce quickly replied. He was almost petrified looking at her lay there.

"What kind of pills, sir? Is she breathing?"

"She is, but just barely. Can you send somebody quick please? We're in room 147, all the way on the end on the front side as you drive in. What do I do? She's burning up." He had purposely avoided her first question just as most others would have done.

"Sir, stay calm. As long as she's breathing, she'll be okay until the paramedics get there. They should be there in less than two minutes, sir."

Bryce couldn't get anything other than a light moan out of Lisa. The only thing that he could pray for was that she wouldn't die. He had never been remotely close to being in any situation like this one. He hurried to clean up as much as he could before the ambulance arrived. He threw all of the tobacco away, poured out the last of the liquor, and sprayed some of her perfume that was lying on the counter to mask the smell.

Suddenly, red flashing lights lit up the room through the thin, dark blinds. As he quickly surveyed the room once more before he rushed to open the door, he saw the bag of ecstasy pills lying on the floor between the two beds. He snatched it up quickly and stuffed the bag in his pocket just as the EMTs knocked.

Bryce let them in and they quickly started checking her vitals. He was glad that they had finally made it there, but he had forgotten to try to put some clothes on her. Lisa was laying there completely naked. He became afraid when he heard one of the men say that Lisa overdosed on something and needed to get to the hospital right away.

As they rushed to get her on the stretcher, one of the EMTs asked him what kind of pills she had taken. Bryce finally decided that it was in the best interest of her health to tell them everything that he knew. He told them that she had taken ecstasy, but wasn't sure how many. Bryce grabbed her belongings, and rode in the back of the ambulance with her. She was in terrible shape.

Once they arrived at Columbus County Hospital, they rushed Lisa inside and directed Bryce to sit in the emergency room waiting area. As he sat there, one of the intake nurses sat down with him and asked him a series of questions so that she could fill out all of the necessary paperwork. Sadly, the only information that he could provide was her name and the kind of pills and alcohol she had consumed. He purposely omitted the fact that she heavily smoked marijuana that day. He didn't want to make things worse than they already were. All he could do was wait and pray for the best result.

Every few minutes he would go to the desk and ask the nurse if she had heard anything about Lisa's condition. All they told him was that she was stable and would be fine. He paced the room all night worrying about what would happen to her. Two hours later, an older man and woman came running into the emergency room asking for Lisa. Those were her parents. The nurse led them straight to her room. The doctors had just cleared Lisa to be seen by her family shortly before they arrived.

Two Sheriff's deputies walked from the back accompanied by the intake nurse that questioned him about Lisa earlier. Bryce's life was about to change. He could feel it in the pit of his stomach. As they walked towards him, he knew they were going to question him about the ecstasy pills. Unfortunately, he had been so worried about Lisa that he didn't remember he still had the bag of pills in his jacket pocket.

"Young man, we need you to follow us outside."

While the deputies escorted him outside, the intake nurse grabbed Lisa's bag and pocketbook and took it to her room. When they got outside, the deputy asked Bryce for his identification and asked him to turn and face the wall. The other deputy thoroughly searched him, and pulled the bag of pills right out of his pocket.

"Mr. Lennon, you're in a world of trouble right now, son. What in the hell were you thinking sleeping with a fifteen-year-old girl and giving her drugs and alcohol?" the deputy sternly asked.

When Bryce heard what the officer said, he nearly fainted. He was immediately handcuffed and taken to the county jail. He had no idea that Lisa Taylor was fifteen. That was preposterous to him. But now, the damage was done. That damn painting.

# Chapter 3. Forever Love

It wasn't unusual for Bryce not to come home at night on the weekends. Sometimes he would spend the night with his friends if it had gotten too late so he wouldn't disrespect Mrs. Minnie. Alexia and Deon were sound asleep when the phone rang that night, but Mrs. Minnie was up early praying for the strength to tell her grandchildren about their mother.

It was 4:22a.m. She didn't have to guess what it was. Any call coming in at that time of the morning meant that something was wrong. And if something was wrong, then it had to be Love.

"Hello?"

"You have a call from an inmate at the Columbus County Jail. You will be billed nine dollars and ninety-five cents for this call. To accept charges, please press 1." Mrs. Minnie accepted. She was floored when she heard Bryce's voice on the other end.

"Bryce?? What in the world?? What happened baby??"

"I messed up Grandma. I didn't know she was underage! They got me down here! They charged me with sleeping with her, a whole bunch of drugs charges…It's really bad, Grandma."

"Let me throw on some clothes real quick. I'll be right there. What in the world, Bryce??"

"No!! They haven't even given me a bond, Grandma. I'd tell you to come if I didn't do anything, but I did it. I really did it. Wait until Granddaddy gets back. I'll call you tomorrow and let you know what's going on."

Bryce hung up the phone before Mrs. Minnie had a chance to say anything else. Mrs. Minnie couldn't go back to sleep after that. She felt like she was going to have a heart attack. She called her father a few times, but he never answered. She wanted to call Love, but didn't think it would be wise to put any additional stress on her. She spent the next few hours doing what most grandmothers in the South would do when they didn't know what else to do- pray.

Mr. Riggs returned her call around 5:30 that morning on his way back from Smithfield. He couldn't believe what she was telling him about Bryce. His entire life he had managed to stay out of trouble. There had to be a reason behind what had happened. When Mrs. Minnie hung up the phone, she could no longer keep her eyes open. She fell asleep sitting upright on the couch in the living room.

Like every other morning, Deon was the first to come downstairs. When he saw his grandmother sleeping on the couch, he made his way into the kitchen to pour him a glass of orange juice. In the quiet of the morning, he heard his grandfather's truck pulling into the driveway outside. Moments later, Mr. Riggs came through the front door and headed towards Mrs. Minnie's room. He was startled when he noticed Deon in the kitchen.

"She's right there sleeping on the couch. She must have stayed up real late watching TV, Grandpa," Deon whispered as he pointed to his grandmother on the couch.

Mrs. Minnie woke up when she heard them. She and her father sat down on the couch and talked for a few minutes about what Bryce told her as Deon sat at that kitchen table drinking his orange juice. Deon knew something was wrong, but knew that he was not to ask questions when adults were talking about something important.

By the time Alexia had come downstairs that morning, they had already called the county jail. The deputy who answered the phone gave them as many details as he could. In a town as small as Whiteville, the deputy knew most of the families that resided there and didn't mind bending the rules for them. The first thing that he told them was that Bryce didn't want to speak to anyone. It would be Monday morning at his first appearance in court before they would be able to see him.

Mrs. Minnie sat Alexia down and told her about what had happened with her brother. She was speechless. They argued all of the time, but she loved her brother to death. The news of Bryce's arrest

113

spread around the town quickly that day. Mrs. Minnie and Alexia found their phones ringing constantly. Of course, most of the people that were calling only wanted to find out the details about the arrest. No one really showed an interest in Bryce's well being. It upset Mrs. Minnie and Alexia to see how inconsiderate people could be, but that is the way things were.

Mr. Riggs took Deon back to his house for the day. They spent the rest of that evening watching movies. Mr. Riggs was worried about his daughter. With so many things happening at once, he could only imagine how heavy her heart was. Deon was unaware of everything. It was best that way.

The detectives did an intense investigation. They found the marijuana, the cigar tobacco, and the empty liquor bottles. Antoinette was the one who signed for the room. She and Brittany were both eighteen-years-old and grew up in the same upper-middle class neighborhood as Lisa. They had been close since they were small children. When the detectives questioned Antoinette and Brittany, the girls admitted that they were all in the hotel with Lisa and that Bryce came over. However, they didn't admit that the marijuana and alcohol in the room belonged to them. They certainly didn't admit that the ecstasy pills were theirs. Their alibi was that they had left Lisa in the room to spend their evening at Ivey's, a local sports bar that everyone went to on Friday nights. They told the detectives that they didn't have any idea that Lisa had taken any pills, smoked weed, or drank any alcohol. They told them that Bryce had been there earlier and left right before they headed out for the night.

Those girls were deathly afraid of their parents finding out that they weren't the decent women that they thought they had reared. They told them that they paid for the hotel because they wanted to spend some time with Lisa because she was so stressed about her cheating boyfriend. They just wanted to help her get him off of her mind.

When they questioned Bryce, he didn't say one word. They told him that Antoinette and Brittany had already told them everything. Bryce continued his silence. Mrs. Minnie called one of the best attorneys in town, Ryan Roseboro, to represent Bryce. Mr. Roseboro went down to the jail to speak with Bryce that evening, but Bryce was almost as silent with him as he was with the detectives. The longer Bryce sat in that jail, the more it dawned on him that he had made the biggest mistake of his life. Mr. Roseboro went over all of the information he had gotten from the detectives with Bryce. Bryce told him the details of the evening, but even with those details, Mr. Roseboro knew that it would be extremely hard to defend him.

Bryce's arrest was the biggest story on every news station that covered the area. Mrs. Minnie and Alexia were not surprised when they saw his face on the television that night. They both sat down in the living room and watched the news together anticipating the dreadful story. As soon as the segment ended, Alexia's cell phone and Mrs. Minnie's house phone began ringing every few minutes. They refused to answer any of the calls. Alexia became more upset each time her phone rang, and eventually just turned it off before storming upstairs to her room for the night. Mrs. Minnie wanted to disconnect the line, but wanted to be available just in case Bryce called. She went to her room to lie in her bed. She was tired, but she couldn't sleep.

Mrs. Minnie tried calling Love in the early hours of the morning, but Love didn't answer. She still hadn't told the children that Love was sick. That stayed on her mind throughout the night, but she knew that she couldn't tell them just yet. She didn't have a clue about when would be the best time.

Mr. Riggs and Deon arrived at Mrs. Minnie's house bright and early the next morning just as she was setting the table for breakfast. Mrs. Minnie sent Deon upstairs to get his sister. He could hear the loud music coming from her room, so he banged loudly on the door.

"Alexia, Grandma said come on downstairs. It's time to eat!"

"Tell her to put me a plate to the side. I'm not really hungry right now."

Deon ran over to Bryce's room not knowing that he hadn't been home. When he ran back downstairs and told Mrs. Minnie that Alexia wasn't hungry, he immediately asked about his brother as he sat down at the table with them.

"Grandma, where's Bryce at?"

Mrs. Minnie didn't know what to tell him and couldn't think fast enough to satisfy Deon. She looked to her father to intervene. Mr. Riggs always knew how to handle things like that.

"He had to go handle some important things with his business this weekend. He'll be back in a few days. I forgot to tell you that yesterday," Mr. Riggs said. Mrs. Minnie stretched her hands to her father and Deon. It was time for their morning prayer.

"Lord,

We come to You this morning as humbly as we know how. Lord, please put Your arms around this family in our time of need. You know our situations, and we're putting them before You so that You can handle them the way You see fit.

Amen"

The prayer that morning was rather short compared to the usual length of Mrs. Minnie's prayers. As soon as Mrs. Minnie said Amen and opened her eyes, Deon was staring at her from across the table with a blank face. She knew right then what was about to happen.

"Is everything okay, Grandma?" Deon asked.

"Everything is okay...There's just a whole bunch of stuff going on right now. Eat your food, baby."

None of them went to church that day. After eating, Mr. Riggs went home. Alexia never came down that morning. When Mrs. Minnie went up to check on her, she heard her music coming from the door. She didn't even bother to knock. She decided to go back downstairs and start cooking dinner. Deon's curiosity grew as the day progressed. They never missed church. And it was abnormal for Alexia not to come downstairs at all during the day. He wanted to ask Mrs. Minnie about what was wrong, but he didn't want to bother her. Mrs. Minnie would explain everything to him when the time was right. He took advantage of the time away from church to play his video games in his room.

Early that evening the doorbell rang. Deon came running downstairs. He knew it was around the time that his mother usually came over. He ran right pass Mrs. Minnie as she walked to open it. He swung the door open, and sure enough, there was his mother standing there with the biggest smile on her face. She hugged and kissed her baby before stepping inside. Mrs. Minnie gave her a hug as well, as soon as she came in.

"Mama what has that boy…"

"We'll talk about that in a little bit, Love. Come on in the kitchen and help me. We'll talk about it," Mrs. Minnie quickly said, interrupting Love before she could say anything about Bryce in front of Deon. They sent Deon upstairs to play his games so that they could talk.

Love appeared somewhat downtrodden. Her hair looked like it hadn't been washed in months. Love had lost so much weight. The light smell of alcohol seeped from her pores. Mrs. Minnie would normally make a slightly sarcastic remark to Love about her drinking, but today was not the day to bring that to her attention.

"Mama, what in the world Bryce done did? I know my baby. There's no way he did that. They got him charged with drugs, having sex with that 15-year-old girl, and whole bunch of other crap, Mama."

"Love, I don't know what's going on and we aren't going to be able to see him until Monday morning when he goes in front of the judge. He hasn't called back since he called that first time and the lawyer I got for him says he doesn't want to speak to anybody. All I know to do is pray for him and see exactly what's going on tomorrow morning."

"I just don't understand. They say that girl is just as hot in her pants as some of them floozies up the street. The thing that really gets me is the drugs. Bryce ain't doing any drugs, and he definitely ain't selling any."

Alexia actually heard her mother when she came in. She wasn't excited about her being there. She never was. It gave her more of a reason to stay in her room. Mrs. Minnie and Love talked about everything from Bryce to Diondre to the cancer. Love was doing a lot better than Mrs. Minnie thought she would be. Mr. Riggs and Mr. Harry Lennon's parents came to the house. Everyone loved those Sundays at Mrs. Minnie's, except Alexia.

When the table was set and everyone was ready to eat, Alexia finally came downstairs. She hugged everyone, but made sure not to sit next to her mother. Love was disturbed by Alexia's attitude towards her. She wanted so badly to bond with her daughter, but because she had neglected those children as long as she had, that was the only way Alexia knew how to feel.

"Lexy, Mr. Floyd asked about you the other day. He wants you to tutor his daughter a few days out the week. That extra money will be good for a few days out the week, huh?" Love asked.

"I spoke to him already," Alexia quickly replied. She kept her head down as she ate. The last thing that she wanted to do was make eye contact with her mother. Everyone at the table got quiet when Love spoke to Alexia. The mood was always tense when they spoke.

In an attempt to break up the monotonous moment, Mr. Harry Lennon's father immediately interjected. "I think we're going to go ahead and retire next month. It's best we go ahead and do it while we have a few years left to do a little traveling before we get too old."

"You can't retire yet. Who's going to preach?" Deon quickly asked. Everyone at the table was shocked at the news. But Love's eyes were still fixed on Alexia.

"I know that church is going to miss y'all when y'all go. Things aren't going to be the same there without you," Mrs. Minnie said as she smiled at Mr. and Mrs. Lennon. They had preached in that community for so long. Everyone knew it was time for them to retire in their old age. Just as Mr. Lennon was about to respond, Love suddenly got up from the table and walked out of the kitchen into the living room.

Everyone's eyes followed Love as she walked out, except Alexia's. No one really knew what to say.

"What's wrong, Mama?" Deon asked as he hurried behind her into the living room.

"Nothing D. I'm not feeling too good, baby. Sit down here with mommy and watch TV." Love turned on the television and embraced Deon as he sat down beside her. Alexia was the next one to try to leave the table. Mrs. Minnie couldn't take it any longer.

"Hold up, Lexy. Love, you and Deon come on in here."

"I'm good, Mama. I'm just not feeling too well."

"No! Get that attitude out of your voice. I am still your mother. Y'all come on in here now, Love. Lexy you can go ahead and sit back down."

Mr. Riggs and Mr. Harry Lennon's parents calmly sat as Love, Deon, and Alexia went back to their seats. Alexia rolled her eyes and let out one of those common teenage sighs as she flopped back down into her chair. Love did the same, almost simultaneously.

"I'm tired of seeing y'all two like this. Y'all can't even be in the same room and act like y'all are civilized," Mrs. Minnie sternly said.

"Mama that don't be me and you know that. That's your granddaughter."

"It don't matter who it is, Love! Right now, we all need to be closer than we've ever been. Deon go upstairs to your room, baby. We'll come get you when we get finished talking."

Deon slowly made his way out of his chair and headed upstairs. Mrs. Minnie waited until he was out of the room before she continued.

"Alexia, you have to stop being disrespectful to your mom. You weren't raised to be like that. And before you even think about opening that smart mouth of yours to say something, I know you don't think you're doing anything to be disrespectful. But child, just because you don't come out of your mouth and say anything wrong or do anything wrong doesn't mean nothing. That little slick stuff like rolling your eyes and the rest of that crazy mess is

125

disrespectful. Point. Blank. Period. God doesn't like that mess," Mrs. Minnie said as she stood behind her chair focused on Alexia.

"Now we all know what's going on with Bryce right now. Y'all got to get this messy stuff together. Life is too short. You get one mama, Alexia, and when she's gone that's it. Me and my mom didn't get along too well, and when she left here, there wasn't a damn thing I could do to go back and tell her that I was sorry!"

Mrs. Minnie was furious at this point. Mr. Riggs and Mr. Harry Lennon's parents were as quiet as church mice while she scolded Love and Alexia. When they heard her curse, it resonated throughout each of them. Alexia looked at her grandmother with a blank stare. They had discussed her ill feelings she had towards her mother more than once. What Love said next would change everything forever.

"It's my fault, Mama," Love quietly spoke as she tightened her eyes closed and took a deep breath.

"I should have been here, right Lexy? I shouldn't have made no mistakes and been the perfect mom like all the rest of your friends got."

"Love, don't," Mrs. Minnie softly said as all of the air came out of her spirit. She did not intend to make Love upset.

"No, Ma. It's okay. I wasted my whole damn life away on drugs, Lexy. Drugs came before you. I put drugs before your brothers. I couldn't raise my own damn children because I made the decision to be a damn crack head!" Love screamed as tears began rolling down her pale cheeks. The built up frustrations of their torn relationship could be felt in every word spoken and seen in every tear that flowed from her beautiful eyes.

Alexia glared at her mother with her crossed arms tight enough to crush an unopened soda can. Alexia tried so hard to be angry, but the tears that flowed from her pouted face said otherwise. The wiser ones in the room, Mr. Riggs and Mr. Harry

Lennon's parents, sat patiently and allowed life to take its course in that moment.

"You ain't gotta worry about me no more, Lexy. As much evil as you got in your heart about me, I know you probably wish I died a long time ago-overdosed, murdered or something. You never in a million years would have guessed that your mama would die of cancer huh? All the mistakes I done made, all the things that could have-should have happened. Just don't make sense that something as natural as cancer could happen to your good-for-nothing mama. I'm sorry y'all. I'll be at the courthouse in the morning to see what's going on with my son."

Love stormed out of the kitchen and quickly walked out of the front door slamming it behind her. No one tried to stop her from leaving.

"What is she talking about?" Alexia asked, looking around the kitchen at their saddened faces. "When were y'all going to tell me, Grandma?" Alexia quickly got up from the table and ran upstairs to her room, slamming the door behind her. As they all sat in the kitchen consoling Mrs. Minnie, Deon's voice brought the room to silence.

"Is Mama going to die? And what's happening to Bryce?" he asked. During all of the chaos that was going on in the kitchen, no one noticed that he was sitting at the top of the stairwell listening carefully to every word.

It was time. Mrs. Minnie sat Deon down and explained what had happened to his brother. When dealing with a young man such as Deon, it was best to be straight forward. They all knew that he was going to ask many questions, and they were all prepared to help answer them. Deon sat attentively as his grandmother explained Bryce's situation.

"So Bryce got caught up doing the nasty with a girl who didn't tell him how old she was?" "Yes, Deon. And some other stuff," Mr. Riggs replied.

"…And they found drugs too. Wow. It's not looking good for him. But what's this about my mommy having cancer? Is she going to die?" Deon

129

looked at all of them sitting there hoping that one of them would answer his question. They were each hoping that the other would answer him. After a brief moment of silence, Mr. Harry Lennon's father spoke.

"Deon, you remember that time I got you that puppy, it was about two years ago?"

"Yeah," Deon said as he positioned his head to the side in confusion. He was trying to figure out why Mr. Harry Lennon's father was telling him this story. He was only concerned about his mother.

"Well your grandma didn't want you to have it because she knew that if anything ever happened to that puppy, you would be upset. And we all knew that something was wrong with that puppy before I got it for you. You looked your grandma right in her face and told her that we're all going to die one day. Then you told her that it didn't matter if anything happened to it. You just wanted to enjoy it while it was living. Deon, I might be an old man but I remember that clear as day because since you said that, I always use it as an example when they have me preach at funerals. So yeah son, we're all going

130

to die one day, really don't matter when, but we all should enjoy each other while we're here. Your mama is real sick right now and the doctors are taking good care of her. Don't worry 'bout nothing but enjoying her right now."

"Yes sir," Deon said right before running back upstairs to his room.

That night was long and lonely for everyone. When Mr. Riggs and Mr. Harry Lennon's parents went home, Mrs. Minnie washed the dishes and put them away alone. She was glad that Love was able to get all of her thoughts out in the open, and even happier that everyone now knew what was happening in their family. The only thing left to do was to pray and meditate on God's Word.

Love cried herself to sleep early that night. Alexia, Mrs. Minnie, and Deon had done the same. Each one of them dealt with the news alone in their own way knowing that the next morning they would have to be in court to support Bryce.

# Chapter 4. Embracing the Last Goodbye

*God,*

*I don't know what's going to happen. I don't know how I got here and in this mess, but I do know that You love me. I was wrong. I should have never did what I did. I should have never even went over there. Lord I'm not saying that I didn't do nothing wrong. To be honest God, I was dead wrong. I just ask that You forgive me. I gotta pay for what I did. I'm a man about mine, but please God...Don't let anybody else have to suffer with me, especially not that girl, her family, or mine.*

*Amen*

After Bryce finished praying in his small cell, he lay on a cold steel bed and awaited his first appearance in court. He hadn't uttered one word to anyone there. The few words that he spoke to the detectives and his lawyer weren't enough to send him home without being charged. And quite honestly, he wanted to be punished. The thought of fifteen-year-old Lisa Taylor's near death experience was troubling him to the core of his soul. He was a young man of outstanding moral character; that's how Mrs. Minnie raised him.

When he was transported to the courthouse, he had an opportunity to meet briefly with his lawyer. He still opted to say nothing. He was the most frustrating client Ryan Roseboro had ever encountered. To make matters worse, Lisa Taylor's father and the district attorney, Chris Matten, were close friends. He and the other inmates who were present for their first appearances were escorted into the courtroom with both their hands and feet shackled and seated in a designated area in the front of the room.

Bryce kept his head down from the time he entered the room. He was embarrassed, but in a brief moment when he lifted his head to take a glance into the audience, he saw that his family was there. Love, Mrs. Minnie, Deon, Mr. Riggs, Mr. Harry Lennon's parents, and to his surprise, Diondre, were all in attendance. Everyone was there except for Alexia. Diondre came into the courtroom late and sat on the very back row. Lisa Taylor's parents were in the courtroom as well. The look of anger on her father's face and the hurt in her mother's eyes as they glared at him for that split second sent a chill throughout his body.

As each case came to a close, it became very obvious that the judge wasn't in the best of moods on that Monday morning. Bails were either being set unexplainably high or not granted at all. Throughout the proceedings, Love's cough resounded in the courtroom. It became so bad that the judge even stopped to ask if she was okay.

When Bryce was called to the front, he and his attorney stood before the judge and heard the long list of crimes that Bryce was being charged with. As they stood there, Bryce leaned over and whispered in his attorney's ear. Mr. Roseboro's eyes widened as he took a noticeable deep breath in front of everyone.

As soon as they entered into a plea of not guilty, the strangest thing happened. No one in that courtroom could have anticipated what happened next.

"Your Honour, at the request of my client, we are asking that the court forgo bail and that Mr. Lennon remain in custody until trial."

"Mr. Roseboro, I've heard a lot of things in my years in this courtroom, but this is by far the strangest request I've ever encountered. At the defendant's request, he will remain in the custody of the Columbus County jail until trial, which is set for October seventeenth. As the judge banged his gavel, Love quickly got up from her seat and exited the courtroom. She didn't even glance at Diondre when she passed him."

Diondre made his way out of the courtroom with the rest of the family leaving not too long afterwards. He tried his best to catch up with Love before she left the building, but she was moving too fast. He knew that woman better than anyone. The look in her eyes said that she didn't want to talk or be bothered with anyone. The only thing Love wanted to do was go somewhere and be alone. She needed to find a way to cope with what had just happened. He looked all over for her when he stepped outside the courthouse. She was already long gone. As he stood on the steps of the courthouse, he heard a small voice that was all too familiar to him.

"Daddy!" Deon screamed as he ran ahead of the rest of the family towards Diondre.

Diondre picked him up and gave him the biggest hug any father could ever give his son. Regardless of Diondre's shortcomings, Deon loved him anyway. Deon didn't care that he was in and out of jail. He didn't care that he rarely showed up for Christmas, birthdays, or even on the days that Mrs. Minnie allowed him to come visit. He loved Diondre as if he were the best father in the world.

"Daddy, why does Bryce want to stay locked up? The judge probably would have let him go right?" Deon asked.

Mrs. Minnie and the rest of the family walked out of the courthouse just as Diondre was about to answer. Mr. Riggs and Mr. Harry Lennon's parents spoke to him kindly like always. Mrs. Minnie's face stiffened in disgust as it always did when he was present.

"Come on Deon. We gotta go baby. You'll see him later on okay. Come on now." Mrs. Minnie grabbed Deon's hand and led him away down the steps. She didn't even look at Diondre. Deon looked back at his father and smiled.

"I'll stop by tomorrow after I get off work, D."

Mr. Riggs quickly began talking to ease the awkward moment. "Diondre, if you got a few minutes and don't mind, I need your help at the house. That old TV in the living room finally gave up the ghost and I gotta get it out of there." Diondre agreed as his eyes followed Deon and Mrs. Minnie as they walked across the street to the parking lot.

"C'mon son. You'll see him tomorrow," Mr. Riggs said.

137

After telling Mr. Harry Lennon's parents goodbye, they made their way to Mr. Riggs' home. Diondre blankly stared out the truck's passenger window during their ride. The thought of Bryce being in jail consumed him. He had spent many nights in that same jail and knew all too well what his son was going through. Diondre and Mr. Riggs did not utter one word to each other on their trip to the house. It wasn't that they disliked each other. It's just that sometimes silence is the best therapy when the right words won't come easily.

It didn't take them long to move that old television outside. Mr. Riggs helped as much as he could, but he was in no shape to be of any real assistance in his old age. Diondre was more than capable of handling it on his own, and that gave Mr. Riggs a little more time to think about how he was going to tell Diondre what he had driven him to his house to say.

"We got it outside, but what are you going to do with it?" Diondre asked.

"They won't let you take it to the dumpster anymore and the trash guys say I have to take it to a recycling center. I'll figure it out later. I appreciate you Diondre. How much I owe ya'?" he asked as he lowered himself down to sit on the porch steps.

"You don't owe me nothing."

Regardless of how Mrs. Minnie felt about Diondre or how many mistakes he made, Mr. Riggs always treated him with respect. And Diondre admired him. However, it still didn't make it any easier for Mr. Riggs to tell him about Love.

Diondre sat down beside Mr. Riggs with his head down gazing at the ground. His saddened posture spoke volumes. He believed that his son had failed because he had failed him as a father.

"D, one the hardest things to do is to let your kids grow up. They'll make you feel like they can conquer the world sometimes and sometimes you gotta sit back and watch 'em be dumb as a box of rocks. Either way it go you gotta let 'em live."

"I know man, but damn..." Diondre replied as he quickly stood up and walked down the steps. "Bryce ain't built for prison, and ain't a damn thing none of us or the best lawyer money can buy can do about it."

Mr. Riggs appeared unmoved by Diondre's sudden emotional outburst, but he understood what the young man was going through. Mr. Riggs knew then that it was time to tell Diondre what he had really bought him over to tell him.

"D, Bryce is going to be alright, but Love...She's not doing too well right now."

Diondre wasn't expecting him to say anything about her. He and Love hadn't spoken in months. Diondre still loved her in his heart, but he had fallen out of love with her years ago.

"The doctors found cancer, Diondre. She's been sick for a while now and finally went to get herself checked out. It's not good at all D. It's not good at all. I can't even sit here and lie to you. It's stage four."

Diondre turned around and started walking away. He had heard rumors that Love had AIDS, but he knew it wasn't true. He had been tested every time he went to jail and his results were always negative. People knew she slept with some of the nastiest men around town to finance her drug habit, and figured that she must have been dying from AIDS to be that sick for so long. He would have never guessed in a million years that the love of his life would end up with cancer.

Mr. Riggs tried to call Diondre back to sit down, but he never turned around. Mr. Riggs couldn't do anything but watch Diondre fade into the sunset. There wasn't any point in keeping it from him any longer. He knew he had done the right thing, and no one could have convinced him otherwise.

Diondre knew very well that they could no longer be together, but that didn't stop him from loving her. She was the love of his life, and just as beautiful to him then as she was when they first met in their high school cafeteria. He walked across town without speaking one word to anyone. The Monday newspaper had been released with Bryce's face on the front page. When Diondre made it to Love's apartment, everyone was surprised to see him. He rarely went to the projects unless he was buying cocaine. Seeing him at Love's apartment was even rarer. He would speak to her if he saw her outside, but they would never engage in long conversation. The one thing that he would do was tell her that he loved her every time he saw her. That always brought a smile to her face.

He banged on her door so long that he became the center of attention for everyone who was outside. They saw her walk in a few moments earlier and were wondering if she would open the door for him. After about two minutes of knocking, Love swung the door open.

"Why you banging on my door like that? I had to throw on some clothes." It was obvious she had been crying and the sight of Diondre only made it worse. Right as he stepped inside, she burst into tears. He wrapped his arms around her and held her small frame as close to him as he could. That embrace meant the world to her. At that moment, Diondre was her rock.

"Our baby, D..."

"Baby, Bryce is young enough to make mistakes and get back on track. This won't last forever. I'm worried about him, but I know for a fact he's gonna be alright. But I can't live without you, Love."

Love softly pushed Diondre away and looked up at his face as a single teardrop rolled down his cheek. He tried to wipe his face before she had a chance to see him crying, but he was too late. That was the first time she had ever seen his eyes water.

"I was going to tell you, but it's just so much that's been going on."

"It's okay baby." Diondre kissed her forehead and wrapped her in his arms again. Her tears stopped and the room was suddenly quiet. She needed him to be there and he knew it. They spent the rest of the day together talking about their children and reminisced on all the good times. They avoided talking about Love's diagnosis. There were a lot of tears that day, but far more smiles.

The rest of the day was hard for Alexia. Everyone in school was extremely nice to her, even her teachers. By then, all of them knew about Bryce's arrest. People didn't confront her about it, but judging from the stares and the whispers, she knew her brother was the hottest topic on campus.

While she was at her locker, a few of the boys came over and told her that they knew Lisa Taylor.

"Three of my dudes from Lumberton smashed her over Christmas break, Lexy. She told them that she was eighteen! They got her drunk and had her on camera and everything after the Christmas tournament. It's a couple dudes here at school that done smashed her. She lied to them about her age too. She ain't nothing but a trick!" Marcus said. He was one of the popular seniors at school. Most of the boys that were in his circle were older than he was, so he knew something about everything that was happening in Whiteville.

The guidance counselor at school saw Alexia towards the end of the day and asked her if everything was okay. Alexia lied and told her everything was fine. She had a long day and did not want to be bothered by anyone. It was hard enough knowing that everybody was talking about her brother behind her back. As soon as her friends dropped her off at home that evening, she ran straight to her room and cried herself to sleep.

The entire family was depressed that night. Mrs. Minnie, Alexia and Deon stayed in their rooms. Mr. Riggs spent the night at home looking through old photos of him and Mrs. Amy. Love fell asleep in Diondre's arms that night. Bryce stared at the ceiling of his small cell thinking about how poor of a role model he had been to Deon. The next few months would be the hardest the family had ever endured.

Mr. Harry Lennon's parents did as they said and retired from the church. A young pastor from the area by the name of Jerome "Smiley" Williams stood in their place. He was an ex-drug dealer from town who had changed his life for the better three years prior. His life-changing moment happened not too far from Mrs. Minnie's house. One night, some young hoodlums robbed him for a kilo of cocaine and shot him three times. They thought that they had killed him, but he survived. When he recovered, he gave his life to Christ and vowed that he would dedicate the rest of his life to Him.

When he became the pastor, the congregation quickly grew larger than any Mr. Harry Lennon's father had experienced. Drug dealers, crack heads and prostitutes were coming and giving their lives to Christ. Pastor Williams was a handsome young man who could stand at the front of a congregation and deliver heartfelt messages that would touch the spirits of everyone in the room. He reminded Mr. Harry Lennon's father of himself in his younger days. Everyone loved him, especially the women. Each Sunday the front pews of the church were filled with flirtatious women, but they soon found out that he was genuinely focused on preaching The Gospel.

Pastor Williams was a breath of fresh air to everyone in the community, except Diondre. If everyone knew his reason, they probably wouldn't blame him. Smiley used to sell cocaine to Love and Diondre all of the time. When they didn't have any money, Love would sleep with him in exchange for drugs. Diondre didn't care. And Love

146

didn't care either. All they wanted was to chase their first high.

It wouldn't have been so difficult for Diondre to deal with Pastor Williams had he not had reason to believe that he could possibly be Deon's father. Deon was conceived during a time where Love had been sexually involved with him. Diondre knew that she had sex with him a lot more times than she told him. Actually, Diondre knew that Love slept with a lot more people than she told him about too, but as long as she was bringing drugs home, he didn't care. Every time Diondre saw Pastor Williams, he couldn't help but think that he could be Deon's father.

In those months, Mrs. Minnie, Mr. Riggs, and Deon showed up every Sunday for church. Alexia stopped going to church altogether right after Bryce was put in jail just as her mother had stopped going when Mr. Harry Lennon died. Love would come to church at least one Sunday each month and sit on the last pew. Everyone could tell that she was there by the sound of her chronic cough. It would echo

147

throughout the sanctuary. People couldn't believe that a lady that small could produce a sound so loud. Little did they know, her cancer was progressing.

As for Bryce, he still refused to talk to anyone. He didn't put one name on the visitor's list. Each week, he would receive letters from everyone in his family. He would read them all, but would never respond. Each week Ryan Roseboro would come to the jail to go over his case with him. Bryce still would not say one word. Mr. Roseboro wasn't getting far with Bryce's lack of cooperation, but Mrs. Minnie was paying him entirely too much for him not to put forth his best effort.

As Bryce's trial approached, the gray cloud over their family just continued to darken. Mrs. Minnie was stressed beyond measure and had to go back and forth to her doctor for her blood pressure. Alexia just shut down. The once straight A student suddenly had grades that dropped to slightly above average. She stopped participating in all the extracurricular activities she was involved in. And to add to it all, she never came out of her room.

The table that once hosted the entire family for breakfast each morning was now only frequented by Deon and Mrs. Minnie. They still began each day with a prayer. Deon made sure to say a special prayer for his mother and his brother. Sundays, however, stayed almost the same. After church, Mr. Riggs would always come for dinner, but Mr. Harry Lennon's parents would often get invited to eat dinner elsewhere. Since they had retired, more and more families asked to have them over for dinner. As for Alexia, she would come down and eat alone once everyone had left the kitchen.

Love's health deteriorated faster than her doctors expected. The chemotherapy treatments took a hard toll on her body. She was barely nincty-five pounds and was forced to shave off all of her hair and wear wigs. At that point, she knew that she was dying and would have to make the most of the time she had left.

The one thing that changed for the better during this time was her relationship with Diondre. He would stop by and spend hours with her whenever he had the chance to. No matter how bad she felt, he was always able to put a smile on her face. He loved to see her smile. It made him feel as though he was making a difference in the small amount of time she had left.

Usually when he came over, he would make sure that all of the chores were done. He made sure every room was spotless. She didn't like him doing all of that work around the apartment, but couldn't deny that she loved his company. And like always, he would kiss her and tell her that he loved her each time before he left. She never wanted him to leave, but it was best that he did.

Every other Saturday, as scheduled, Diondre came to Mrs. Minnie's house to see Alexia and Deon. That was the one time that Alexia would come out of her room. On those Saturday mornings, both Deon and Alexia would run to the door as soon as they heard the bell ring. Mrs. Minnie would stay in her room while he was there. She would look out into the living room to make sure that they were doing okay. Because Mrs. Minnie had her issues with Diondre, it made her angry to see those children so happy to spend time with him. He had never done anything for those kids. And she believed in her heart that Love would not have been so bad off if she had never gotten involved with him so many years ago.

On this one particular Saturday morning that Diondre came, Deon was still sleeping. Mrs. Minnie heard the knock at the door while she was in the kitchen cooking breakfast, but intentionally didn't answer. She hoped that he would get tired of standing there and leave. The more he knocked, the louder she turned up the volume of the gospel radio station she was listening to. The solid thump of him knocking traveled up to Alexia's room, and she hurried downstairs as soon as she heard it just as she had always done. When she rounded the corner, she noticed that her grandmother was standing in the kitchen. She broke stride to give her an evil look before opening the door for her father. Mrs. Minnie simply rolled her eyes and continued to cook breakfast.

As soon as Alexia opened the door, the bitter stench of alcohol crept up her nostrils. There Diondre stood leaning against the frame of the door with his face resting on his raised arm. He was crying profusely. This was the first time she had ever seen her father like that. At the sight of Alexia, he took a deep breath and began to speak.

"She's dying baby," he softly whimpered as he stumbled forward towards Alexia and embraced her. She was overwhelmed by the smell of cheap liquor as she stood petrified in her father's arms. Mrs. Minnie rushed to the door at the sound of Diondre's weeping.

"What happened Diondre?" Mrs. Minnie asked as she stood in the hallway. Diondre slowly looked up at Mrs. Minnie and loosened his embrace.

"Dear Lord, Diondre. What's wrong?" Mrs. Minnie sternly asked again.

"She's dying, Mrs. Minnie. The doctor told her she got three months. Maybe even less." As soon as the doomful news spewed from his quivering lips, he fell to his knees and continued to sob as he leaned against Alexia's small frame.

Love found out the previous day and told Diondre when he came to visit later that night. She sat him down calmly on her couch and told him what the doctor said. Surprisingly, it wasn't an emotional confession. She appeared to be at peace with her fate. Diondre, on the other hand, couldn't bear the news. He knew that sadness was the last thing Love needed to be surrounded with at a time like this. So he left and spent his last few dollars on crack and alcohol until he was too drunk to bring the bottle to his mouth.

Alexia couldn't believe what she had just heard. As much as she disliked Love, the news her father just gave them brought sudden tears. Mrs. Minnie slowly slipped back into the kitchen before Alexia or Diondre could see her cry and immediately began to pray for the health of her daughter and the strength of her family.

Diondre knew it was best that Deon not see him in so much sorrow. So he told Alexia that he would leave before Deon woke up. He did not want to be forced to explain what was happening with his mother. When Alexia walked back into the house, she could hear Mrs. Minnie praying softly as she walked past the kitchen. She hurried to her room. Just as she shut her bedroom door, Deon burst out of his room and rushed downstairs anticipating that his father would be coming soon.

Mrs. Minnie quickly finished her prayer when she heard Deon's little feet rushing downstairs. As soon as he entered the kitchen, Mrs. Minnie was sitting at the table smiling at him. Her face was damp and red, but filled with joy at the sight of her grandson standing in the doorway. He brought her peace in that moment.

"Grandma, when my daddy comes over today I want to go help him clean my mama's place. He always goes over there after he leaves here. I might as well help him this time. Can I please?"

"Baby, an emergency came up and your daddy ain't gonna be able to make it today. He called earlier, but we're going to go see your mama in a little bit okay?"

Deon's sudden look of disappointment quickly changed when Mrs. Minnie told him that they were going to visit his mother. Deon was so excited that he didn't even ask when breakfast would be ready. He ran straight to his room to get dressed so that he could see his mother.

Mrs. Minnie got up from the table and finished cooking. Her only concern was making it to Love's apartment to check on her. There were many thoughts going through her mind as she frantically hurried to wrap the food in aluminum foil for Alexia to eat later on that morning. Mrs. Minnie knew better than to ask Alexia if she wanted to go with them to see her mother. There was no use in asking.

It didn't take long for Mrs. Minnie and Deon to get ready. They left the house and headed to see Love. Deon was so excited about going to see his mother that he didn't care how dangerous Mrs. Minnie was driving. She was usually cautious, but that day she sped and didn't come to a complete stop at each stop sign. Deon didn't mind it though. He had always thought Mrs. Minnie drove too slowly anyway.

When they pulled into the driveway, Mrs. Minnie noticed that Pastor Williams' car was parked in front of her place. As they walked towards the front door, they saw Pastor Williams embracing Love on his way out.

"God has it all in control Love. It's gonna' be alright," Pastor Williams said as he embraced Love. When he turned around, he saw Mrs. Minnie and Deon standing there.

"Good morning, Mrs. Minnie. Hey there, Deon." Deon ran past Pastor Williams without acknowledging his greeting and wrapped his arms around his mother's waist.

"Mama, I was going to come over with daddy, but he had an emergency or something. C'mon, we're going to help you clean up." Deon grabbed Love by the arm and pulled her into the living room.

"Pastor, we just decided to come over this morning and check up on her," Mrs. Minnie said. After Deon and Love had moved away from the door, she felt much more comfortable telling him the truth about them being there.

"Pastor, it's a trying time you know. Diondre came by the house a little earlier and..."

"Mrs. Minnie, I know. I can see it all over you right now. Love called me about five o'clock this morning and told me what's going on so I came right on over." At that very moment Mrs. Minnie couldn't hold a straight face any longer. All of the muscles in her face tightened and she burst into silent tears. Pastor Williams placed his hand on her shoulder to comfort her.

"Love is fine, Mrs. Minnie. She's more worried about y'all than she is anything else. That's what we been talking about all morning. C'mon inside Mrs. Minnie. It's best she go ahead and get it all out in the open with you while I'm here."

Pastor Williams led Mrs. Minnie inside and closed the door behind them. Love and Deon were in the kitchen washing her dishes when they walked in. When she heard the front door shut, she walked into the living room and told Deon to keep washing.

When Love came into the living room, Mrs. Minnie and Pastor Williams had sat down on the couch. Mrs. Minnie walked over to her and hugged her. For the first time since Love found out the grim news, she cried.

The three of them spent the next few hours talking and praying together. Love instructed Deon on how to clean each room. He really was trying his best to help his mother, and understood that whatever they were talking about in the living room was really important so he tried not to bother them.

While they were there, Mr. Riggs stopped by Mrs. Minnie's house. When Alexia heard his truck pulling into the driveway, she made her way downstairs and opened the front door so he wouldn't think that anyone wasn't home.

Mr. Riggs knew something was wrong the minute he looked into Alexia's eyes. As he made his way to the porch, she came outside and sat on the steps so that they could talk.

"Lexy, where'd your grandma get to this early in the day?"

"They went to my mom's."

Mr. Riggs hadn't heard Alexia refer to Love as her mother in years. It shocked him to hear her say it. Alexia stared across the front lawn as he made his way to the chair on the porch refusing to make eye contact with him. Just as he sat down, a plane flew just above the clouds over the house.

"I hate them damn things. Everybody in the world thinks it's the fastest way to get there. But once you add up getting to the airport two hours early, going through them long lines checking your stuff in, and then all the time it takes to get off and get your bags, you could of just drove wherever you were going."

"That's the only way you can get to London, China, or anywhere across the ocean, Grandpa."

"I stopped thinking about going to places like that a long time ago, baby. Amy begged me to take her to Paris for years. I always told her I was too busy, but hell; I could have made more than enough time if I really wanted to. I'm stubborn. Always have

159

been. Now my whole life done passed away and I'm too old to even want to go anywhere, Lexy."

"You're not too old, you just don't want to."

"Every day I get a little older, Lexy. The things I didn't give a damn about turn into regrets day by day...I should have taken her."

Alexia turned around to look at him. By that time his eyes were fixed in the same manner that hers were just moments before. He felt her looking at him, but didn't turn his head to look at her.

"The quicker you start giving a damn about things that you should, the less regrets you'll have later on, Lexy. I use to say that Amy left before I had a chance to make up for all the things I did wrong. The truth is, I had the chance every day while she was here."

Mr. Riggs and Alexia looked at each other for the first time since he had arrived. His soft smile said everything he couldn't find the words to.

"Tell your grandma and Deon I stopped by. I gotta get to Smithfield to handle some business. Hopefully I'll be back in time to make it to church in the morning." He got up from the chair and made his way to his truck. He didn't want to sit there long enough for Alexia to see his eyes water. That always happened when he thought about Mrs. Amy. He left before Alexia could tell him about what Diondre had told her that morning about her mother.

Soon, many had found out about Love's illness. It was rare for someone so young in town to be diagnosed with cancer. Love was indeed terminally ill, but many people believed that it was just a rumor.

From that point, Diondre spent most of his time with Love. As soon as she opened her eyes in the morning, he would be staring at her waiting to help in any way he could. He only left when he found a small job to do around town that would put some funds in his wallet. Once again they were inseparable, and had fallen in love for what would be the last time.

Mr. Harry Lennon's parents, Mr. Riggs, Mrs. Minnie and Deon would stop by each day. Usually, when Mrs. Minnie came over, Diondre would leave to mow someone's lawn or do some hustle he could find. But he would not leave until he spent time with Deon. They cherished every moment together. Deon chose to believe that his parents would be a couple again so that they could live together as a happy family.

Deon could tell that things were changing in spite of everyone going out of their way to make sure that he was unaware of what was happening with his mother. Alexia still made no attempt to mend her relationship with Love. She never went to visit, but would speak to her whenever she came by the house.

Everyone coped in their own way. Diondre would often sneak away from Love every few nights to get as drunk and as high as he could. He never had to go far. There were more than a few drug dealers in the projects who were always willing to serve him anything he wanted. Love was thankful for all of his help, so she pretended that she didn't know what he was doing.

Mrs. Minnie stayed busy by taking Love to her doctor's appointments, running errands, and homeschooling Deon. She spent the few free moments she had in her room praying. Some of her prayers lasted for hours. She believed in her heart that God would perform a miracle for her daughter if she prayed hard enough.

The elders, Mr. Riggs and Mr. Harry Lennon's parents, handled their family's situation very well. Although they did have a hard time coping, the beauty of old age made things a little easier for them. They had lost many people near and dear to their hearts throughout their lives. They had grieved enough to know that there was nothing they could do but to allow God's Will to be done.

The hurt that they were feeling was unimaginable, but they appeared to be well composed to those who didn't know what they were going through. The only one who was truly happy was Deon. At times, seeing him happy was all they could hold on to.

# Chapter 5. Unfathomable

Each week the family made attempts to contact Bryce. They continued writing letters, sent messages through his attorney, and even made attempts to see him in person on visiting day only to find that Bryce hadn't put one single name on the visitation list.

Bryce sat in his cell and completely cut himself off from the world. The only time he parted his lips to speak was when his attorney came to the jail to update him on his case. Even then his words were few. The day Ryan Roseboro told Bryce that his mother was dying was one of the most heart-wrenching moments of his career. His heart ached for the young man. He had never in his life been given the duty of delivering that type of news to anyone. Bryce showed no emotion as Ryan sat across the steel table in the cold room in the county jail and told him. He blankly looked into Ryan's eyes for a moment before he stood to walk out. When the deputy opened the door to escort him to his cell, he looked back at Ryan.

"Tell her I love her and I'm okay"

As soon as Ryan walked out of the jail he called Love and delivered the message. At that point, it didn't matter that Bryce hadn't spoken with any of them since he had been put in jail; it brought her joy knowing that he was okay. Every dying parent who cares about their children always wants to know that when they leave this earth their children will be okay.

Leading up to Bryce's trial, Love's condition grew worse as did Diondre's habit. The worse she got, the more crack cocaine Diondre used. He helped her with all that she needed during the day, but would sneak away as soon as she closed her eyes for the night. Sometimes he wouldn't show up until the next morning. When he got there, he would find Love asleep on the bathroom floor most times. Those are the nights where she would go to the bathroom in the middle of the night and not have the strength to make it back to her bedroom. He would apologize every time, but that never stopped him from leaving to go get high in the middle of the night. Love hated it, but put her anger to the side to have him in her presence.

On the Sunday before the trial, Love called Mrs. Minnie early that morning. Her coughing was worse than it had ever been causing Mrs. Minnie to believe that something was terribly wrong. Surprisingly, the only reason she was calling was to tell her that she and Diondre wanted a ride to church. That made Mrs. Minnie smile. When Mrs. Minnie told Deon that his mother and father would be attending church that Sunday, he insisted that she call Love back and ask her what she was wearing so that he could wear a matching outfit. Mrs. Minnie laughed at him and told him to hurry upstairs to get dressed so that they could leave. Deon didn't go upstairs before grabbing the cordless phone from the living room so that he could call his mother.

"Hello," Love answered as she struggled not to cough.

"Mama, what are you going to wear to church?" Deon whispered. Love's cough quickly turned into laughter. Laughing made her pain worse, but at that moment it was well worth it.

"Baby, why you whispering? Grandma don't know you on the phone do she?"

"Shhh. What you wearing Mama? Im'ma get in trouble if she comes up here and I ain't getting ready. Tell me, Ma," Deon whispered while he peeped out of his bedroom door towards the stairs to see if Mrs. Minnie was coming.

"Baby, I'm going to wear that red dress I got."

"Dang! Okay. I'll figure out something. Bye." Deon whispered before quickly ending the call.

Love laughed and went to tell Diondre about the conversation she had just had with Deon. He smiled. It was perfect timing. At a time like this he needed to smile. Truthfully, they both needed to. Diondre used to love going to church, but ever since Pastor Williams started preaching, he had not taken one step into the church. He was cordial with Pastor Williams in public, but secretly, he couldn't stand the ground he walked on.

While Love waited for Diondre to get dressed, she couldn't help but think about how sweet it was of him to agree to go to church that morning. Although she knew they needed all the strength and prayers they could get for Bryce, she also wanted to be as close to God as she could before she passed to make sure she made it into Heaven. Diondre loved her more than anyone in this world, and she knew it pained him to see Pastor Williams. When Diondre walked out the room, she looked up and saw her knight in shining armor looking better than he had looked in years.

"Baby I might can't get around like I used to, but if one of them hussies in that church look at you too long I'm goin' to get up and slap her into the Holy Spirit."

"You might as well slap 'em soon as we walk in because you already know they goin' to look," Diondre replied as he walked over to her and kissed her before sitting down beside her.

"D, when I'm gone you gotta get yourself together, baby. Those kids love your dirty draws and they need you, especially Lexy. I let 'em down. It's too late for me, but you got time."

No sooner than Love finished talking, they heard the sound of Deon's little fist banging on the front door. When Diondre opened it, Deon ran straight pass him to hug his mother.

"Hey daddy," he said as he ran to hug his mother.

"I didn't have anything red that was clean to put on, but look," Deon said. He wore a black suit, white shirt, and black tie. He pulled up the bottom of his pants to show Love his bright red socks. Deon managed to make it out of the house without Mrs. Minnie seeing them. Surely she would have made him change had she known.

"Diondre! Do you see this child!?!?" Love asked as she laughed and hugged Deon.

Suddenly, she began to cough. That's what normally happened when she did too much in a short

169

amount of time. It was obvious that she was getting worse. When she removed her hands from her mouth, she saw spots of blood in her palms. She quickly wiped her hands and mouth to make sure that Deon or Diondre didn't see it. They tried to help her, but she insisted that she was okay.

When she made it to the bathroom, she cleaned up with a cloth and placed it into the hamper. She looked in the mirror as she washed her hands and saw a woman who was dying. Most times she felt as though she was doing well on the chemotherapy treatment, but the blood was a quick reminder of her situation. Recently, those reminders seemed to come more frequently. When she came out of the bathroom, Diondre and Deon were waiting at the front door for her. She hid her pain behind the biggest smile she could manage and got in the car with her family to head to church.

They all sat on the front pew that morning as a family. The only two people that were missing were Alexia and Bryce. If they were there, the family would have been complete. However, they were happy that the majority of them were there together to worship Christ on Sunday morning.

Pastor Williams titled his sermon, It Doesn't Matter What Happens, He's in Control. He preached from his soul that day and had everyone in the congregation clinging to every word he said. Every point he made was relevant to the lives of each person sitting in the pews that morning. At one point, Love looked over at Diondre and saw moisture forming in his eyes.

"…And what if God doesn't come save the day? What you goin' to do? Stop believing and trusting in him? It's women out here who keep forgiving ole good-for-nothing men for cheating on them over and over, but walking 'round with they mouth poked out because God ain't show up when they thought He was supposed to. Men walking 'round here with they mouths poked out because some situation or another ain't turn out like they wanted it to. With all that He's done, how can anybody in their right mind be upset with God about anything?!? Folk kill me with that

171

mess. You know what?? I done figured it out. A lot of people don't really want God. They want Superman or Batman." Pastor Williams preached like that would be his last sermon.

At the end of the sermon he called everyone to the front of the church to pray for the Lennon family. He anointed each person's head with Holy Oil. The piano player was playing a soft melody that evoked tears throughout the sanctuary. When Pastor Williams stepped in front of Diondre, he stared into Pastor Williams eyes. After anointing his head with oil, Pastor Williams leaned over and quietly whispered something into Diondre's ear. Whatever he said caused Diondre to immediately shut his eyes and grip Love's hand a little tighter.

When church ended, everyone made their way to Mrs. Minnie's house. For the first time in years, they had all been under the same room at the same time. While Love, Mrs. Minnie, and Mr. Harry Lennon's mom prepared dinner, Diondre went upstairs to spend time with Deon and Alexia. Mrs. Minnie became upset when she saw Diondre walking upstairs. Before she could make it out of the kitchen, Mr. Harry Lennon's mother stopped her. Love was too busy to notice what had happened, and it was best she didn't. In spite of everything that was wrong in their lives at that moment, Love was happy that day. She took Pastor Williams' sermon to heart. Mr. Riggs and Mr. Harry Lennon's father sat on the porch talking and laughing as they did most Sundays.

When dinner was ready, everyone sat down at the table and ate until they were full. There was enough food to feed a small army. Most importantly, everyone in that room was genuinely happy. Love and Alexia didn't speak that much to one another, but Alexia went over to hug her mother as soon as she walked in the room. Their eyes would meet every so often and that warmed Love's heart. Diondre and Mrs. Minnie, on the other hand, didn't even look one time at each other.

The end of the evening produced a moment that was unexpected from everyone. As Mr. Riggs prepared to leave, he offered to take Love and

Diondre home. While Love was saying goodbye to everyone, Alexia hugged Diondre and then turned to Love and hugged her again. And then the unthinkable happened.

"I love you, Mama"

That day was one of the most beautiful days the family ever had together, with the exception of Bryce. That night as everyone laid happily in their beds, Bryce was thinking of his day in court that was less than twenty-four hours away. He knew then that the only thing he could do was leave it in God's hands.

Ryan Roseboro was falling apart. In all of his years of practicing law, he had not ever worked a case as difficult as this one. The District Attorney made an offer that would have sent Bryce to prison for at least seven years. In addition, he would be registered as a sex offender for the rest of his life. He paced back and forth in his office for hours each day before the trial. After reviewing all of the evidence, he had given up all chances of winning the case. His client wasn't any help, the news was biased, and the trial had become the biggest story in Whiteville media's history.

On the day of the trial Ryan Roseboro called Mrs. Minnie. It was early in the morning and she was already down on her knees in her ritualistic prayer.

"Good morning, Mrs. Minnie."

"Good morning, Ryan. We'll all be there around 8:30 this morning. Is that too late?"

"Not at all...Mrs. Minnie, I've done all I know how to do. There's no way possible for me to do anything for him. I don't have the balls to sit here and lie to you and tell you that there's going to be some kind of miracle today. I'm not taking any payment from you Mrs. Minnie. Bryce tied my hands at the first appearance. I'm sorry, but we're going to have to take the plea."

"Sweetie, I knew that a long time ago, but I figured if there was any hope for anything you would be the one to do it. We're going to be there for him, and you're going to walk out of that courtroom today with your head high. And you can kill that nonsense

175

about me not paying you. Your time is just as valuable as anyone's. We'll see you in the courtroom at 8:30 am today, Ryan."

"Thank you, Mrs. Minnie."

The family met on the steps of the courtroom that morning shortly before the proceeding began. Everyone was there, including Deon and Alexia. It was inevitable that Bryce would be going to prison. With the way he had refused to allow anyone to see him since he had been arrested, they feared that it would be a long time before they would ever see him again. They all knew that it would be the last time he ever saw his mother.

When they entered the packed courtroom, there were reporters standing in every corner. As expected, Lisa Taylor's family along with a multitude of supporters was there to watch Bryce's demise. The room quieted as the family made their way to the front. Every eye in the room was fixed on them. Lisa Taylor kept her head down, with the exception of the brief moment that she looked up and met Alexia's stare. The rest of Bryce's family made a conscious effort not to look in her direction. Lisa could do nothing but lean into the arms of her father.

Ryan Roseboro and Bryce entered the courtroom escorted by guards. The courtroom immediately fell silent. The decision had already been made that Bryce would take the seven-year plea. Regardless of the young man's fate, the family was there to provide him with the support he needed.

During the hearing, Deon didn't look at anyone other than his older brother. He hoped that Bryce would turn to at least look at him, but he never did. Bryce didn't glance to look at anyone who sat behind him. There was no need for testimonies. Bryce had already accepted what was going to happen. When the judge banged the gavel, Bryce was sentenced to seven years in prison. Before the guards escorted Bryce away, Love made her way to the front of the courtroom calling out to him with Deon on her heels.

"Please, I just want to hug him."

A shackled Bryce reluctantly broke his stride and turned to see his frail mother in tears. Unnoticeable to the rest of the courtroom, the judge nodded his head giving the guards permission to allow Love to embrace her son.

He made his way towards her and allowed her outstretched arms to embrace him. With the side of her face pressed against his, her warm tears ran down the side of his cheek. That brief moment was just enough time for her to whisper words that he would hold onto for the rest of his life.

"I Love you, baby."

"I'm sorry, Ma." That was the last thing he said before he was escorted away. Deon stood there beside his weeping mother as they watched his big brother being taken away. Love was the only one who he chose to look at that day. Sadly, it would be the last memory he shared with the most beautiful woman in his life.

The following months were horrible. Alexia somehow found a way to blame everything wrong in her world on Love. In her heart, she wished that she was born into a different situation. She began to hate Love again, and it showed. She stopped acknowledging Love's presence at family dinners on Sundays. The words 'I love you' were never said again to her mother after Bryce was sent to prison, but she refrained from being disrespectful.

Mr. Harry Lennon's parents traveled the world in their retirement. They would call home at least once a week to check on everyone, but they were more concerned with living their lives as if they were on an eternal honeymoon. Diondre used more drugs as Love's condition worsened. And the more Love's condition worsened, the less she saw of him. Oftentimes, she would wake up and struggle to the bathroom in tears knowing that he was out in the middle of the night trying to find crack cocaine.

Mr. Riggs was the strongest of the family. He continued to conduct his business in Smithfield. He spent more time at Mrs. Minnie house. She and those children needed a constant male presence at the house that they could depend on. His daughter had always been strong, but this situation could be mentally stressful for anyone. Mrs. Minnie became so worried about her family that she stopped going to church as often as she used to. She and Deon would watch sermons that they could find on television. Although Alexia was dealing with the same problems as everyone else in her family, she continued to grow more distant from everyone.

Deon would write letters to Bryce each week telling him how everything was going in his life. His big brother never responded. He didn't even call. Deon always ran outside to the mailbox anticipating Bryce's letters. It didn't take him long to realize that Bryce would never write back. He was heartbroken.

Love's cancer had completely consumed her body. Each doctor's visit deposited more bad news into her spirit. She was numb and had begun to lose all hope. She was less than one-hundred pounds, and spent most of her days in the bed. Deon and Mrs. Minnie stopped by to see her every day, but Love hated for Deon to see her like that. She begged Mrs. Minnie not to bring him over as often as she did, but Mrs. Minnie denied her daughter's request. Alexia eventually decided that she needed to visit her mother. She would accompany Deon and Mrs. Minnie a few times a month. She never did anything other than hug her, but she came. She would always use her schoolwork as an excuse to not spend any time with her mother.

One day Love was awakened out of her sleep by the worst pain she had ever felt in her life. Love knew that her days were short, but her pain scared her into believing that she may have had less time than she was originally told. She called her mother and asked her to take her to see her oncologist. Usually, Mrs. Minnie would bring Deon with her to see his mother, but there was something in Love's voice that made her leave him at the house with Alexia. As soon as Mrs. Minnie pulled in front of Love's apartment, she rushed in to put her in the car so that they could get to the hospital. The oncologist explained that her pain meant that her condition was worsening. It was that day that Love and Mrs. Minnie decided that it would be best for her to spend her last days in hospice care in Myrtle Beach, South Carolina so that she could at the very least be comfortable.

# Chapter 6. Here I Die

Mrs. Minnie, Mr. Riggs, and Diondre brought her belongings to the hospice facility ahead of time in efforts to make her living quarters as personable as possible before she would arrive. Mrs. Minnie would have preferred that Diondre not assist with the moving process, but Mr. Riggs wanted his help. The two of them only spoke when it was absolutely necessary, and Mrs. Minnie did everything in her power to avoid him.

Mr. Harry Lennon's parents stopped traveling so much to spend Love's last days with her in Whiteville. Mrs. Minnie hired a nurse to come to Love's apartment each day to care for her until she was scheduled to leave for the facility. Alexia took charge of babysitting Deon while her grandparents and her father transported all of her mother's possessions.

Alexia had been depressed ever since she found out that her mother had a tentative date for her death. She was hurt knowing her mother would leave this earth before she would be able to have a relationship with her, but was also upset because she believed that years of hard living led to her demise. Those thoughts made it impossible for Alexia to ever make peace with her mother. The tears she cried were a mixture of anger, regret, and grief. There were no words that could describe the tornado of emotions that whirled inside of her.

While Mrs. Minnie was away, Deon became curious as to why his grandmother had not been home. He went to his sister to find out where she was. Alexia had been so overwhelmed that she could not even think of the right words to say to him. She told him that as soon as Mrs. Minnie got home that night he should go and ask her. As soon as Deon heard his grandmother pull into the driveway, he rushed to the door to find out what was happening with his mother. Mrs. Minnie answered every question he asked the best way she could until he could not think of any other questions to ask. When they

184

finished talking, Deon appeared unaffected, but that wasn't the case at all. He was just as distraught as any kid would be after learning that they would soon lose their mother to cancer. However, in his mind, he was the man of the house and had a responsibility to be strong for everyone.

The night before Love went to the facility Mrs. Minnie was up late in the living room packing a few things so that she and Deon could spend a few days with Love. She heard a room door open and then feet hurrying downstairs. When she looked towards the staircase, she saw Alexia making her way to the refrigerator to get something to drink. After grabbing a bottle of water, she sat on the other end of the couch in the living room to talk to her grandmother.

"Lexy, you should come on down with us a few days."

"Grandma I'm riding down there with you, but who's coming back tomorrow that I can ride home with?"

185

"Everyone is coming back tomorrow night except your dad, Deon, and I."

Alexia started to get up to go to her room, but Mrs. Minnie quickly stopped her.

"Hold on, baby." Alexia took a drink of her water and slowly sat back down on the couch.

"Baby, she's going to be gone forever here shortly and there's not anything anybody is going to be able to say or do to ever bring her back. You have an opportunity to cherish these last few moments with her, Lexy. I didn't get that chance when my mom decided to blow her brains out," Mrs. Minnie firmly said. Alexia sat there staring straight ahead into Mrs. Minnie's eyes completely emotionless.

"I'm going down there Grandma, but what's the point of me staying? You and everybody else know that if she wasn't dying she'd be out smoking crack and tricking like she's been doing her whole life! I just don't see the point in acting like she deserves a whole bunch of damn sympathy!" she screamed. Mrs. Minnie immediately slapped her on her left cheek before she could say another

186

word. Alexia closed her eyes for a split second, and then looked back into Mrs. Minnie's face, appearing nonchalant with what she had done.

"Grandma, I'm sorry. But for me, it's the truth. I'm the only person that has to wake up and go to sleep with my feelings. And I get slapped for telling you how I feel?"

"I didn't slap you because of how you feel, young lady. I slapped you because I've told you time and time again not to curse in my house! If that's how you feel at this point, then I'm going to let you deal with that with God, but she is your mother and the only one you'll ever have. And in less time than you think, she's going to be gone and for the rest of your life. You'll have to deal with the fact that you felt the way that you felt, and what you chose to do with those feelings while she was on her death bed. Go to your room, Lexy! Now!"

Alexia hurried to her room before her grandmother had to tell her again. Mrs. Minnie sat down and thought of the issues Alexia had with her mother, but there was nothing that she could do at this point. She always believed that they would work out their differences later on in life. She figured that there would be enough time. Now that there wasn't, she could only pray that she won't be as hurt as she was when she realized there was no time left to build a relationship with her mother.

After Mrs. Minnie finished packing, she quietly walked upstairs to check on Deon. His bedroom door was slightly cracked and the light from the hallway shined just bright enough to see his small frame. He was snoring lightly and spread wildly across his bed. Mrs. Minnie noticed that he had fallen asleep on top of an open notebook with a pen still clutched in his hand.

Mrs. Minnie walked into his room to take the pen out of his hand and place the notebook on top of his nightstand so that she could cover him up for the night. He never once opened his eyes. Before she left the room, she picked up the notebook to see what he was writing. As she stepped into the hallway, she realized that he was writing a letter to Bryce.

*Dear Bryce,*

*The doctors gave Mama some bad news. She is dying soon so they are moving her to a place at the beach so she can die happy. Alexia is still mad at her. I don't speak to her about Mama because she gets mad. Everybody else is doing good. It's really sad here but I only cry when I'm by myself. I have to be strong since you're not back yet. Do you think mommy is going to Heaven?*

*Love you*

He had fallen asleep before he could finish. Mrs. Minnie quickly put the notebook back on his nightstand and walked to her room so that she could go to sleep. She thought about the question Deon asked his brother in the letter. It was a question that had been on her mind lately. She got down on her

189

knees that night and prayed that Love had made peace with God.

The next morning, Mrs. Minnie made breakfast. As usual, Deon was the first one to make it to the table. After Mrs. Minnie finished preparing breakfast, Alexia came downstairs just in time to hear her grandfather's old truck pulling into the driveway. Mrs. Minnie's face suddenly stiffened.

"Y'all daddy is out there with your grandfather. We have to hurry up." They ate quickly so that they could begin their journey to South Carolina. Mr. Riggs never came to the door. He and Diondre both knew that it wouldn't be a good idea for Ms. Minnie to see him this early in the morning so they decided to sit in the truck and wait.

Just as they were walking out of the house to leave, Mr. Harry Lennon's parents' car pulled up. Deon waved with excitement when he saw his mother sitting in the back seat. It took her a little while, but she waved back at him. Moments later their small convoy left for Myrtle Beach with Mr. Riggs and Diondre leading the way.

Tears fell from Love's eyes throughout that entire trip. She knew it would be the last time that she would see the streets of Whiteville. Each house, each road, and each building that she saw brought back memories. Whether good or bad, each one proved to be as important to her as the other. Every few miles, Mrs. Harry Lennon would turn around to ask her if she was okay. Love didn't say a word, but nodded her head as she wiped her tears away. Each minute that passed felt like a second to Love. Her life was quickly coming to an end, and she knew it. All she could do now was make the most out of the little time that she had left.

When they arrived at the facility, Diondre quickly got out of Mr. Riggs' truck to see how Love was feeling. Shortly after, Deon ran over to the car to check on Love as well. Mrs. Minnie and Alexia went inside to fill out the paperwork so that Love could be admitted. Thankfully, the nurses were already prepared to aid in the process. One of them followed Alexia and Mrs. Minnie out to Mr. Harry Lennon's car so that they could help her into the wheelchair. Love was as weak as she had ever been and needed much help. The nurse rolled her into the facility with everyone following close behind. Deon walked alongside his mother and held her hand until they got to his mother's room.

Once they arrived and opened the room door, Love clutched Deon's hand a little tighter and turned and smiled at him. He walked in the room and looked around amazed at how nice it was. As the rest of the family came in, the nurse and Diondre helped Love into her bed. Deon walked out onto the patio and gazed at the ocean. Everyone was thoroughly impressed with the facility and extremely satisfied with Love's room.

The facility was much smaller than most facilities of its kind. It was suited to host twelve patients at a time. It was much more expensive than other facilities in the surrounding areas because it sat right on the North Myrtle Beach shoreline. It was a peaceful, remote haven that had a clear view of the Atlantic Ocean.

In each room there was a large sliding glass door that led to a small patio area that was decorated with colorful wild orchids and provided a beautiful view of the ocean. Winding cobblestone paths gave the residents and their visitors a short walk from the patio to the shoreline. The smell of the ocean made everything so surreal. It seemed as though the angels had constructed that place. Since watching the sun set was thought to be a constant reminder of the few days that they had left, the facility was purposely designed to face the east so that the patients could watch the sun rise each morning.

Each spacious private suite consisted of two bedrooms, two bathrooms, a large living area next to the patient's bed, and a small kitchen area with a small table for the guests. The patient's bed sat in the large, open living room area just a few feet away from the large sliding glass door that led to the patio. A black, fifty-two inch television was mounted on the wall on the opposite side of the patient's bed. A large half-moon shaped sectional sofa sat in the open area across the room from the large sliding door. The patient's bathroom was close to the patient's bed for easy access. The guest rooms were of a moderate size and shared a large bathroom.

At any time, visitors would be able to sit with her comfortably in the spacious room, which included a full-sized refrigerator, microwave, and a large table. The family could enjoy eating together each day like they did on Sunday afternoons. It resembled an extended stay hotel much more than it did a hospice facility. The cost was well worth it though. Every patient could spend their last moments with their loved ones there in peace.

"Mama this place is amazing," Deon said as he came to Love's bedside. Love looked at Deon and smiled. Diondre softly clutched her hand and looked at his son with joy in his eyes that no one had seen in a long time.

They spent the day laughing and talking about all of the moments they had cherished. Well, almost everyone did. Diondre and Mrs. Minnie did their best to stay as far from each other as possible. Mrs. Minnie put her and Deon's things away in one of the rooms, and occasionally came out for moments at a time. Diondre put his few things in the other guest room. He quickly went back out and stood close to Love's bed when he was finished.

Everyone had been interacting with Love to make her feel special, except Alexia. She was extremely distant and played on her phone the entire time. She only spoke when she was spoken to, and even excused herself on occasion to go out on the patio to make phone calls. Soon, she left the room and walked down the cobblestone pathway to the edge of the shore. That was Deon's chance to get close to the ocean. When Alexia realized that she would have to keep a close eye on him, she extended her conversation. She decided that it was better for her to spend time outside watching Deon play than to sit inside the room with her mother. When Alexia and Deon came back inside, she made an attempt to be cordial with her dying mother.

Just before nightfall, Mr. Riggs, Mr. Harry Lennon's parents, and Alexia said their goodbyes.

They all hugged and kissed Love before leaving, including Alexia. And that surprised everyone. Whether she was sincere or not, that action had brought an extra piece of joy to the room that evening and added the finishing touch to Love's new and final home.

Alexia and Mr. Riggs rode back to Whiteville together that night. From the moment she got in his truck she knew he was going to want to talk to her about the way she had been treating her mother. Alexia pretended to be exhausted so that she could avoid the inevitable. Mr. Riggs knew his granddaughter all too well. To her surprise, he didn't say one word about Love on the ride home, but decided that he would spend the night with her at Mrs. Minnie's house. They said goodnight to one another after they made it in the house and were asleep as soon as their faces hit their pillows.

Deon, Diondre, and Love stayed up talking for as long as they could. Shortly after the rest of the family had left, Deon snuggled into the bed with his mother. He talked to her until he fell asleep. Diondre was drifting in and out of sleep in the chair beside the bed as Mrs.

Minnie was fighting sleep on the sofa. It had been a long day for all of them. Love was just about to slip off into her own dreams when she heard a light knock at the door. It was one of the nurses.

"Hey, Love. I'm the night nurse assigned to you, sweetie. I'm Kye," she softly said as she quietly walked into the room. Diondre and Mrs. Minnie woke up when she walked in. She politely introduced herself to each of them and explained that she would be on night duty for the duration of Love's stay.

Kye was a beautiful, brown-skinned, young lady with short hair who looked to be about thirty-five years old. She didn't stay long at all. She just wanted them to know that she would always be available every night for the duration of Love's stay if they ever needed anything.

One of the things that made the facility unique was the scheduling of its nurses. There were two nurses that were assigned to each patient that was admitted - one for the twelve-hour day shift and one for the twelve-hour night shift. They would be responsible for the patient they were assigned to until he or she passed away. At the patient's point of death, those two nurses would go on leave for at least thirty days and get a new assignment after that period. The nurses were scheduled this way so that the patients could become comfortable with having the same nurses during such a difficult time. Each of the two nurses lived at the facility during their rotation. The work was very demanding, but they were more than generously compensated for their time.

Diondre helped Deon out of Love's bed and put him next to his grandmother in one of the guest rooms. That's where Mrs. Minnie and Deon retired for the night.

"Is mommy okay, daddy?"

"She's good, D. Get some sleep son."

Diondre slept on the chair next to Love's bed and held her hand until they both fell asleep.

It was dead silent in there that night. Right before Mrs. Minnie went back to sleep, she cracked the window so that she could hear the soft sound of the ocean. It made everything seem so peaceful.

Kye came to check on Love a few times throughout the night. Each time, Diondre would wake up out of his sleep at the sound of the door opening. He would look over to check on Love and then turn to nod at Kye to let her know that she was okay. Kye would smile and quietly shut the door so that she wouldn't disturb Love's sleep. The moonlight shined through the sliding glass door and illuminated the entire room. Diondre watched over Love all night while she slept. The moonlight shining on her face made her appear to be as young and beautiful as she was when they first met. Thinking about their childhood brought him a sense of joy that he would hold on to for the rest of his life.

The warmth of the sun woke Love out of her sleep the following morning. No sooner than she opened her eyes, she began to cough horribly. Her health had drastically changed from the previous night. Mrs. Minnie dropped her Bible onto the bed and rushed into the room as soon as she heard her daughter's horrible cough.

Mrs. Minnie stood on the other side of the bed rubbing Love's back. Love had rolled over towards Diondre as she coughed in her bed sheets. Diondre grabbed a bottle of water from the refrigerator and waited to help her drink it once her coughing had slowed. The sight of blood spewing from Love's mouth caused Diondre to pick up the phone immediately and page the nurse. Mrs. Minnie couldn't believe what she was seeing.

Deon came out of the room just in time to see the day nurse rushing over to help his mother. She was an older Caucasian woman who looked as though she may have been fifty-five. She was passionate about what she did and made Love's family confident that she would take good care of her while she was there.

"Baby I need you to sit up for me okay," the nurse said as she helped Love sit up in the bed. Diondre and Mrs. Minnie stood back out of her way. The nurse raised the head of Love's bed and gently helped Love lay back against her pillows. Her coughing slowed after that.

"We're going to have to clean all this up sweetie. It won't take long at all." Diondre handed the bottle of water to the nurse and she helped her drink. Deon was worried about his mother and walked to the side of the bed to make sure that she was doing better.

"Go back in the room for a minute baby," Mrs. Minnie said as soon as she saw him.

"Mama you okay?" Deon asked.

"Yes D," Love softly said. Although he didn't want to leave her side, he turned around and went back into the room.

"I'm Sarah. Y'all. Forgive me. I was supposed to get introduced to you all when you checked in yesterday, but I had to run home. By the time I got back I figured it was too late and y'all needed your rest."

After Love's cough had completely subsided, Sarah and Diondre helped her over to the couch so that the bed linen could be changed. Mrs. Minnie knew how bothered Deon could become when he was worried about his mother, so she got him and herself ready for the day.

201

"Grandma, we can take Mama down to the beach later on. I bet it'll make her feel better. There wasn't anybody out there yesterday when me and Lexy went down there. Dang...Call Lexy and tell her to bring my swimming trunks when they come."

"I'll call her in a little bit. We gotta make sure your mom is situated and everything before we even start thinking about that water, D." When they came out from the room, Sarah had changed the sheets and Love was back in her bed talking to Diondre.

Deon always loved to see his mother and father together. He ran over to the side of Love's bed and leaned over with his arms outstretched to hug and kiss her. She gave him the biggest hug and kiss that any mother could have given her son. Diondre and Mrs. Minnie sat down and smiled at the sight.

"Mama, the nurse will be here in a few to give me a bath. She wants you to be here though. Diondre is going to take Deon down to the water for a little while," Love said. Deon ran straight to the sliding glass door before his mother could say another thing. They all laughed at his

202

excitement. He and his dad made their way down the cobblestone path to the beach.

Sarah came in around that time and showed Mrs. Minnie how to properly give Love a bath without having to move Love out of the bed. Although it was painful for Love, it was necessary for her care. Sarah started speaking about herself to take Love's attention off of the pain. She was the widow of an abusive boat dealer whom she loved until his very last breath. They had traveled to many exotic islands and vacationed in the world's finest resorts during their twenty years together, but she was never as happy as everyone thought she was. When he drank, he would beat on her like he was fighting a man. One night, he got drunk at a small bar on a beach that he frequented and made the irresponsible decision to drive himself home. A patrolman spotted his car swerving and attempted to pull him over. The alcohol made him believe that he could outrun the police. As a result of driving drunk over one hundred miles per hour, he lost control of the car, hit a light pole, and died on impact. Shortly after his death, she was hired as a nurse at the facility and had been working there since then.

After they finished bathing Love, the three women continued to become acquainted with each other. In the middle of their conversation, Mrs. Minnie excused herself from the room to walk out on the patio. Love thought that then would be the perfect time to talk to her nurse about what was soon to happen.

"So this is where it happens?" Love said.

"Where what happens, sweetie?" Sarah replied with a puzzled look on her face.

"I'm on my death bed. After all these years I thought it was going to be me getting killed on the street, overdosing or something like that…It's going to happen right here. I'll never speak to my oldest child again, my daughter could care less about me, and Deon is too young to even understand what's going on," Love said as she stared out at the ocean.

Sarah looked over at her and found that a few tears had escaped the corners of her eyes. She grabbed some tissue and handed them to her. She knew from past experiences that being quiet during this time helped patients cope best. Love had suddenly realized that sooner than later she would be confronted with death.

Mrs. Minnie had been outside on the patio attempting to call Alexia. Since she didn't answer the phone, Mrs. Minnie called Mr. Riggs instead. When Mr. Riggs answered the phone she could barely understand what he was saying and their call dropped. She figured that he must have been headed to the facility and was driving through an area where there was poor reception. When she walked back inside, she saw that Sarah had gotten up to leave so that Love could sleep in peace.

Mrs. Minnie looked outside once more to admire the beautiful view. She was mesmerized by it all. Soon after, she spotted Diondre happily chasing Deon up the cobblestone path. To avoid an awkward moment with Diondre, she went into her room and began to read her Bible again. When they walked in and realized that Love was sleeping, they both lowered their voices.

"We gotta be quiet. Mama's sleep."

"I'm 'bout to go take a shower, D. Stay in here and watch your mama 'til I get back."

Deon lay across the sofa and flipped through the channels until he found a cartoon he wanted to watch. At every commercial break, he would get up to go check on his mother. On his way back to the couch, he heard a light tap at the door. It was his beloved grandfather, Mr. Riggs. Deon signaled for him to be quiet and pointed to his sleeping mother. He had brought breakfast for everyone that morning from a diner nearby, and it smelled delicious. Mrs. Minnie had planned on getting something from the cafeteria downstairs, but had not gotten a chance to. She walked out of her room when she heard her father and became instantly upset when she did not see Alexia with him.

"Where's Lexy?"

"She wasn't feeling well this morning when I was about to leave. She popped up early-just wasn't feeling well."

Mrs. Minnie was so disappointed that she tried to call Alexia again. When she didn't answer, she immediately sent her a text message to find out what was wrong. Mrs. Minnie placed her phone back on the couch and went to make everyone a plate. When they all quietly sat down at the table, they joined hands to pray. Mrs. Minnie joined hands with Diondre as she prayed, and squeezed it when she thanked God for bringing them all together. When Mrs. Minnie came to the conclusion of her prayer, Love looked over towards the table and addressed her mother.

"Where's Lexy?" Love asked as Mrs. Minnie walked over to raise the head of her bed up so that she could eat.

"She wasn't feeling well. She's coming with your grandparents later on today or in the morning, baby," she said.

"Mama you know ain't nothing wrong with that girl."

"Just eat baby. Lexy will be here later today or in the morning."

Mr. Riggs and Diondre pretended they weren't listening and continued to eat their breakfast. When everyone was done eating, they talked about anything that they believed would bring a smile to Love's face. Sarah came in and joined the conversation as well. It was apparent that she wanted the family to look at her more as a friend than a nurse.

As the day progressed, Mr. Riggs went out onto the patio to enjoy the sunshine and smell of the ocean. As soon as Deon saw him walking out of the door, he followed right behind him. They watched the ships pass by in the distance and enjoyed the weather that Myrtle Beach had to offer. After a while, Deon had become unusually quiet.

"What's bothering you, D?" Mr. Riggs asked.

"Why doesn't Mama have any machines or any things like that in the room?" Deon asked. Mr. Riggs continued to stare out across the ocean. He was trying to find the right words to answer Deon's question.

"Deon, right before your Grandma was born, her mama got really sick. She was having all these big headaches and complaining about her stomach. I had no idea what was wrong with her," Mr. Riggs said. Deon looked back into the room and saw his mother talking to Mrs. Minnie. She was smiling, and that comforted Deon momentarily.

"See, back in the day people thought the beach had healing powers. The salt in the air was believed to be able to heal just about anything, D. So we packed up and came on down here for a week and had the time of our lives. The headaches and the pains in her stomach all went away by the second day." Mr. Riggs said.

"So you think this is going to heal Mama?" Deon asked.

"D, I might not know a whole lot, but to be honest with you I don't think this place has any more healing power than those prayer cloths them

209

preachers sell on television. But I do know that a change of scenery can take a lot of pain away."

"I don't want her to die," Deon said as he got up and walked over to the door to go inside. Mr. Riggs didn't say a word. There was nothing left to say.

When the sun set that evening, Mr. Riggs and Diondre said their goodbyes so that they could drive back to Whiteville together. Mr. Riggs had volunteered Diondre to help one of his friends move some furniture into a storage building. Diondre needed the money more than ever now. He hugged Deon, told him he loved him, and promised him that he would be back in a few days. Then he walked over to Love and passionately kissed her like he had never kissed her before. He didn't want to leave her, but he needed every dollar he could get. Mrs. Minnie was disgusted at what she had just witnessed, but Deon quietly giggled at her and smiled in approval of his parent's love.

Mrs. Minnie walked the two of them out to Mr. Riggs' truck. She had tried to call and check on Alexia, but yet again, she did not answer.

"Diondre, please go talk to your daughter. That child didn't even have the decency to call me back. This ain't the time for her to be childish, and nothing I say to her makes sense to her. Please talk to your daughter."

"I'll try."

When Mrs. Minnie walked back into the room, Kye was there struggling to get Love back into the bed.

"My God, what happened?!?!" Mrs. Minnie asked as she ran over to assist.

"Somebody decided that she wanted to go out on the patio, and had a whole lot of encouragement from a little person," Kye replied as she smiled.

"Grandma we just went out there so she could get some fresh air."

"I'll grab a wheelchair and bring it back after I finish up my reports," Kye said as she left the room.

"It's okay, Ma. I just got a little weak when I was walking back to the bed. I'm not just going to sit in this bed for the rest of my life," Love asserted.

"I'm not mad at all, baby. You just gotta be careful, Love."

The three of them watched television that night until Love drifted off to sleep. Shortly after, Deon and Mrs. Minnie took their showers and went to bed. A few hours later when Kye was making her rounds, she found Love in her room watching a pastor on television.

"Love, you should get some rest," Kye said as she quietly rolled the wheelchair to the end of Love's bed.

"I can't sleep girl. I've never slept this much in my life and now everybody wants me to sleep the rest of the little time I got away. You might as well watch some of this sermon with me. I ain't going to sleep no time soon."

Kye sat down in the chair beside the bed and watched television with Love. The preacher was as charismatic as any other and spoke with a passion that reminded Love of Mr. Harry Lennon's father in his younger days.

"How long have you been saved Kye?" Love asked.

"I've been saved for a few years now. What gave you the impression that I'm saved?" Kye asked as she briefly took her eyes off the television and turned towards Love.

"What else am I supposed to think? You got that tattoo on your arm as big as day."

Kye looked down at the large cross tattoo on her forearm and slowly ran her hand across it admiring the detailed artwork.

"Look at it a little closer," Kye said as she leaned over to let Love look at her arm. There was a rugged scar that ran down the middle of the cross that was perfectly hidden by her tattoo.

"When I first moved down here from D.C. to go to school, I was broke as hell, girl. I could have gotten a job waiting tables or something, but I swear, I went to every restaurant around and nobody would hire me. All the other girls I was in school with seemed to be doing alright, you know? After a few days here and there of missing meals or not being able to even buy tampons, I started stripping at one of these rinky-dink clubs round here. At first it was just good money and everything was cool, but then I started doing what most girls in that club do.

"Some of those old guys were giving me five-hundred to a thousand dollars to sleep with them. They were flying me out to Vegas, Miami, L.A…It was crazy. But then one night I went home with one of them old jokers I'd met at the club. He'd been tipping me big all night and to be honest, he was actually cute. We went to his house and did what we went there to do, but when I was ready to go, he was too drunk to take me back to my car. I ended up getting a cab and when the cab driver pulled me behind the club to let me out at my car, he raped me.

"Everybody had already left the club. There wasn't a point in trying to scream. Nobody would have heard me. I just cried and let him take it at first, and then I started fighting back. I don't know what got into me because he was way stronger than I was. I couldn't fight him off. But that just pissed him off more. I fought him hard enough just to get him off me, and he pulled a knife out his pocket and tried to stab me. If I wouldn't have put my arms up and tried to block him, he would have probably gotten me right in my throat. Luckily I was able to run to the gas station across the street. He was long gone by the time the police got there.

"My father died a few weeks later. He was the first man who raped me. I was almost ten when it happened. I never said a word to anybody about it. All I could think about while I was at the funeral was not ever being able to tell him that I forgave him before he died. I'd made it up in my mind that I was going to tell him after that taxi driver tried to kill me. I just never had the chance to do it. The cross covers the scar and reminds me of how much God loves me."

As Love lay on her pillow, she placed her hand on Kye's. By the time she finished talking, the sermon had ended.

"Get you some rest, Love."

"I don't feel like I'm dying Kye, but I know. It's happening faster than I thought. When it gets too bad, don't let them let my baby watch me suffer. Please don't let them put him through that."

215

"It's time to go to bed, Love. I'll see you tomorrow." Kye turned out the light and walked out of the room. Love lay in the bed gazing out of the open blinds as the moonlight on the horizon kissed the ocean until she fell asleep.

As for Diondre, he went out in search of some crack cocaine as he had done so many times before. Mr. Riggs dropped him off at Love's apartment earlier thinking that he was going to get rested so he could wake up early the next morning and help his friend, but getting rest was the last thing on his mind. It didn't take him long to find what he wanted. There were more drugs in those projects than anywhere else in town.

Mr. Riggs had planned to talk to Alexia that night after he dropped Diondre off. He stopped by Mrs. Minnie's and let himself inside. He found Alexia on the couch sound asleep and decided to walk into his daughter's room so that he could retire for the night as well.

# Chapter 7. Forever

As Love lay on her death bed, Bryce was suffering at his own hand. Prison had drained all of the hope out of him. He hardly ate anything and only spoke when he had to. In fact, most of the inmates and faculty believed that he wasn't able to speak at all.

He quickly lost thirty-seven pounds, and spent most of his days in bed. His reclusive behavior led to a mandatory psychological evaluation that revealed that he was suffering from severe depression. As a result, he was ordered to undergo counseling sessions on a weekly basis. They were no help. He became more withdrawn each session.

The only person that he considered to be a friend was his cellmate, Mr. Coot. Mr. Coot was an incisive man in his late sixties. He had been in prison longer than most men that were there. He was a tall, built man, but his old age made the newer inmates wonder why so many feared him.

Mr. Coot was originally convicted of shooting his fiancé in her face after he caught her cheating on him. Although she survived, he was sentenced with a long prison term. When he arrived at the camp, he resembled Bryce in many ways. He was withdrawn and didn't adjust very well. He spent all of his time in the weight room or in the chapel. He needed to become stronger just as much as he needed to pray. There was a gang in the prison that would steal from his cell every day. The group even went as far as attempting to rape him. The guards knew what was being done to Mr. Coot, but they never once took action or reported it to the warden.

After a few years of lifting weights, he had developed vengeance in his heart and enough muscle mass to be considered one of the strongest men in there. One night, the guards found five members of the gang that was harassing Mr. Coot, dead in the showers. When the inmates heard what had happened, they all blamed Mr. Coot. Some of guards were sent to detain him for questioning. They found him in the chapel praying while the gang leader's body lay at the altar in the front of the church. Mr. Coot had a devilish grin plastered across his face when they took him away. Although he was charged with the death of the gang's leader, they never had enough evidence to find him responsible for the other five bodies. From that point forward, he was considered the most feared man in the prison.

Each morning Mr. Coot would wake up early and pray. Bryce would never come down from his top bunk to pray with him, but Mr. Coot would pray loud enough for Bryce to hear him. He did the same when he read the Bible. He was a wise old man, and knew that Bryce was listening even though he pretended he wasn't.

After Bryce read letters from his family, he would always throw them away. And each time he threw them away, Mr. Coot would get them from the trash and save them. Sometimes Mr. Coot would read them in efforts to try to convince him to write back, especially to his mother, but he never did.

One night right after the lights were turned off, he nudged the bottom of Bryce's bunk.

"Bryce, you up?" he asked in a sharp whisper.

"What's up, Mr. Coot?"

"I don't like getting in people business young blood, but God been putting it on my heart...You got your own reasons for cutting your family off, but don't make them pay for your mistakes man. That little boy take the time to write you all the time, and you too shamed to understand that you're putting them through more pain by not talking to 'em than the pain you think you caused 'em when you got yourself in here. You killing your mama faster than that cancer is. You can't take back what you did, but you can't hold on to it for the rest of your life either."

Bryce never really opened to Mr. Coot, but he always thought deeply about what was said to him. Mr. Coot grew to like Bryce and was sympathetic towards his situation. For Bryce, Mr. Coot's praying and reading the Bible aloud helped him hold on to the little sanity that he had left. As a result, they had developed a peculiar relationship that mostly consisted of Mr. Coot talking and Bryce listening. Mr. Coot tried to encourage Bryce to forgive himself and allow his family to enter his life again, but the shame of what he had done still burdened his heart. Bryce wasn't ready to forgive himself; even with being cognizant of the fact that his mother was dying.

As time passed, Love told Kye and Sarah more of her life story. They told her about themselves as well. Love had started to become so sick that she could not get out of bed. On her worst days, she was too weak to speak. Mrs. Minnie and Deon never left her side. Most mornings, Deon would wake up before his grandmother. He would sit in the living area and watch cartoons or write Bryce letters until his mother awakened in the morning. On days that he was anxious to talk to her, he would open the blinds so that the sunlight could warm her face. The rays shining through the glass always put a bright smile on her face.

Alexia came every few days with either Mr. Harry Lennon's parents or Mr. Riggs. Each time she walked into the room, it instantly became silent. There was something special about the moments when she walked over to hug and kiss her mother. However, as soon as their embrace ended, Alexia would purposely drift further away from Love as the day progressed. She made sure to either walk her brother down to the beach or sit on the patio talking on the phone with her friends. Everyone attributed it to her being a typical teenager, but Love knew that her daughter still had ill feelings about her. There was nothing that she could do to change her mind, and it was secretly killing her on the inside.

Alexia never spent the night with her mother. She always made a point of saying that someone needed to watch the house. For the sake of peace, no one ever questioned her reasoning for leaving. She departed just as she had come earlier. She hugged and kissed her mother and then told her goodbye before exiting the room.

Diondre was there at least three days out of the week. When he was not there with Love, he would be in

Whiteville finding as much work as he could so that he would be able to have enough money to make it through the week, which included supporting his habit. He gave Love all of his attention when he was there. Not one minute would pass without his hand in hers. They would gaze into each other's eyes and whisper sweet nothings to one another. Of course, Mrs. Minnie was not pleased, but a piece of her was happy to know that her daughter was happy. Deon loved everything about his parent's rekindled relationship. He longed for a complete family all of his life, and it became realistic for the first time in his life at the facility.

Diondre and Deon would go to the beach in the morning before Love and Mrs. Minnie woke up. They would play on the ocean's edge and enjoy the rising of the morning sun. Deon didn't care what they did as long as he was able to spend quality time with his father. They were spending more time together now than they had ever done in his life.

With each moment that Deon gave thanks for his parents reuniting, his mother got worse. No one wanted to believe that the end of her life was as close as it was, but the signs were there. Her fate was inevitable.

Late one night when Kye came by doing her rounds, she found everyone in the room sound asleep except Love. She was surprised to see her awake with the night being as late as it was.

"Love, what are you doing up this late?"

"I'm not ready." Kye could barely hear Love's brittle voice through her tears when she replied.

Kye's heart immediately crumbled. She was taught that allowing a patient to vent without being interrupted was the best thing to do. She sat down in the chair beside the bed and reached over to squeeze Love's hand.

"This ain't how nobody supposed to leave here. Look how I'm leaving my babies Kye. The little girl I always wanted hates me! My son doesn't even care enough to write and let me know how he's doing! Heaven only knows what he's going through. The love of my life is just as strung out as ever, and the only thing I can say I've done worth a damn with my life is have three kids!"

"It's okay, Love. Calm down a little bit, baby. You don't need to get yourself worked up."

"I've disappointed everybody who has ever loved me. It seems like everything is okay when they all come, but it ain't. And it's too late to say I'm sorry, and it's been too late to change what took my whole life to mess up...When they put me in the ground, they're going to stand up and tell a bunch of lies about how good of a person I was. Not one of them is going to say I was a crack head, a drunk, a deadbeat mama, prostitute, or none of that. They're just going to sit up there and lie like they do about everybody."

"Love, it's not too late. You and everybody you care about are still here. And as long as y'all are all still breathing, you got a chance to make everything right that you think is wrong. We serve a God so big, Love. He knows your heart. He knows how it's all

225

going to turn out. You just gotta have faith that He's going to work it out. More importantly, you gotta have enough faith that however He works it out is how it's supposed to be. His plan and how He wants things to go is the only thing that matters Love. You got time to do a lot, but you ain't got time not to trust God."

Kye handed Love some tissue and made sure she was doing better before she left the room. She started to close the blinds, but Love insisted that she leave them open. Over the past few nights, she had grown accustomed to falling asleep as she gazed out at the moonlight over the ocean. She said that it made her feel as though God was directly watching over her. That calmed her.

The next morning, Deon woke up extra early and sneaked out of Mrs. Minnie's room to go into the living area. He tiptoed as gingerly as he could to make sure that he didn't wake his grandmother. When he made it to his mother's bed, he found that she was already awake smiling at him.

"Good morning, baby," Love said softly as she squinted her eyes in pain. Mornings were becoming more painful each day. Some days she would cough uncontrollably when she first woke up, whereas other days she would be in unbearable pain and have to call Sarah to give her medication to ease it for her. Deon came over to the bed just before Sarah arrived on this particular morning. Love did everything she could to hide her pain from Deon.

"Mama, I need to ask you something real important," Deon said as he looked deeply into Love's eyes.

"You can ask me anything D. What's on your mind?"

"Do you really, honestly, believe that there's a Heaven?"

Love began to cough before she could answer. Deon didn't hesitate one second to run into the next room and wake his grandmother. As soon as he reached the door, Mrs. Minnie was already rushing into the room to see what was happening with her daughter. Almost simultaneously, Sarah walked into the Love's room to conduct her morning rounds.

"What happened, baby?" Mrs. Minnie asked as she looked back and forth between Deon and Love.

"We were just talking, Grandma, and she started coughing."

"Do Grandma a favor and go back in the room until we can get your mother better okay?" Deon did as he was told, but didn't take his eyes of his mother until he went inside the room. He hurried to the bed and cried.

Love's coughing was horrible. There was a mixture of blood and dark colored vomit that spewed from her mouth for three excruciating minutes. Deon was relieved when he could no longer hear his mother suffering. He desperately wanted to help Mrs. Minnie and the nurse clean his mother up, but quickly decided against it. Deon believed that it was his question that caused his mother to go through that terrible episode to begin with.

Love was breathing heavily and appeared almost lifeless as Sarah tried to get her back to a comfortable state. Once Love was completely taken care of, she effortlessly fell back asleep in her bed. Mrs. Minnie kissed her daughter on the forehead and then went to check on her dearly loved grandson.

"Your mom's going to probably be asleep for a while, D. She had a really rough time just then."

"I didn't mean to make her upset Grandma."

"That wasn't your fault sweetie. Your mom is just really sick, that has nothing to do with you."

Mrs. Minnie had no idea that Deon had asked his mom such a critical question, and Deon wasn't going to tell her either. He was worried that she would be upset with him for asking. They said their morning prayer and got ready for the day while Love slept.

That day the entire family arrived early. Mr. Harry Lennon's parents picked up Alexia, and Mr. Riggs and Diondre followed right behind them. They had never seen Love so exhausted. They all knew then that it was only a matter of time before she would pass away. Diondre sat down beside her and embraced her hand as always, but she didn't tighten her grip. She was incredibly weak now, and the only thing that he could do in that moment was pray.

Everyone in the room was hurt. Alexia looked at her parents emotionless. The elders quietly talked amongst themselves in a concerted effort not to focus on the sadness that had filled the room.

Alexia walked Deon down to the beach not too long after she had gotten there. As usual, she talked on the phone with her friends to distract herself from her mother's plight while Deon threw as many seashells as he could find into the ocean. The rest of the family went out on the patio and talked over tea, except Diondre.

While Diondre sat there holding Love's hand, Sarah came in with one of the doctors. When the others took notice, they all came into the room. Once inside, Sarah asked that all the adults step into the hallway so that the doctor could speak with them. They hadn't spoken to a doctor since they had been there so they knew that something had to be wrong.

"After this morning, I'm sorry to tell you that you should be saying your goodbyes. At best she has a few days. If there's any other family or person you may want to see her, it's best if they get here now." Before turning to walk away, he handed Sarah a sign to place on the door. It read "Do Not Resuscitate."

Everyone tried to remain strong after the doctor had given them the news, but each of them quietly began to cry. Mr. Riggs placed his arm around Mrs. Minnie. Mr. Harry Lennon's parents embraced each other. Diondre couldn't take what he was hearing. He slowly lowered himself to the ground, and blankly stared at the opposing wall. Although no tears formed in his eyes, he was crushed.

The doctor and Sarah left the family alone to help support one another. Without saying a word, Diondre stood up and went back into the room. When he opened the door, Alexia and Deon were standing by Love's bed looking directly at him. Love slowly turned towards the door and smiled at him. He walked over and kissed her on her forehead. Shortly after, the rest of them came in and stood around the bed. In that moment, the love that Love felt from her family was warmer than the morning sun that had kissed her face each day.

She outstretched a hand to Deon who was standing on one side and to Diondre who stood on the other. Instinctively, each of them joined hands to make a circle so that they could pray.

"This time I'll lead, Mama," Love softly said as she weakly smiled at her mother.

"Dear Lord,

I want to thank you for giving us this time. We thank you for this moment right here. Before you Lord, I lift up my family. Clean our hearts. Make us whole. Before you, I ask that you forgive me for all the wrongs that I've done to everybody in this room. I pray that you allow them to forgive me-even if not now, in their own time. Reach out and touch Bryce's heart. Let him know that we love him. Give him peace. Fix the things in us that are broken. Heal the things in us that can only be healed by you Lord. Forgive us for all of our wrongs. Make us pleasing to your sight.

232

Amen"

It took so much energy out of Love to say that prayer. When she spoke, her voice sounded like a raspy whisper, but it was heartfelt. Each of them hugged and kissed her when she finished. She was far too weak to stay up much longer after that. She fell asleep while the rest of them spoke quietly in the family room. Diondre never let go of her hand, and kept his eyes fixated on her throughout the day.

When the sun set, Mr. Harry Lennon's parents said their goodbyes and left for Whiteville, both afraid that it would be their last memorable moment with Love. Mr. Riggs, Diondre and Alexia decided that they would sleep there that night. Each time Love woke out of her slumber, Diondre was right there watching over her. He told her he loved her every time that their eyes met, and it brought her peace.

Around midnight, Love suddenly woke up and startled Diondre.

"Baby, it's okay," he said as he quickly sat up out of the chair.

"Come hold me," Love whispered.

He carefully got into Love's bed and gently wrapped his arms around her as they watched the moon cast its smile on the ocean. She tightened her grip on his hand and spoke just loud enough for him to hear her.

"You have to quit for them." As quickly as she said it, she drifted off to sleep again.

Throughout the night, Kye peeked in the room to check on Love. Each time she looked, she saw that Diondre was in bed holding her. Not once did she stop to interrupt. She let them enjoy one another as she continued to do her evening rounds.

Before daybreak, Deon woke up and walked to his mother's bed to find his father asleep in the chair holding her hand. Diondre had gotten up out of the bed once he realized that Love was sound asleep. Deon quietly walked to the other side of Love's bed and leaned over to kiss her on her forehead.

"I believe in Heaven, D." He was surprised to hear his mother's voice. His eyes lit up and he kissed her once more.

"But there's another place kind of like Heaven that I bet nobody ever told you about baby," Love quietly said. Deon looked into her eyes. Love was in much more pain than her smiling face showed.

"The sun shines twenty-four hours a day baby. It's the most beautiful blue sky you'll ever see. It and the other stars all stand still over the clouds at the same time. It's so pretty, D."

Deon looked at her in amazement. He had never heard of such a thing in his eight years of living. He was trying to imagine what his mother had just told him. Love's eyes were barely open, and travelled back and forth between Deon and the morning view of the sun rising above the Atlantic.

"It's a huge island that sits on the bottom of an ocean somewhere on one of those planets on the other side of the sun that they haven't discovered yet. That ocean surrounds the whole place, D. If you walk

235

to any edge of the island, you can look right through the ocean walls and see the black little mermaids and all the huge fish swimming," Love whispered as she reached out to hold Deon's hand. Water formed in the slits of her eyes, but no tears fell. Deon was at a loss for words. He was envisioning everything that his mother had told him.

"For miles around, you can sit there and admire how God made it so that the ocean walls surrounding that place don't just crash in on everything. The thick tropical jungle surrounding the city is filled with big, bright, pretty birds and twice as many animals that you will find in the jungles on earth.

"And the city, D...It's filled with tall buildings with big windows that reflect the sight of the ocean wall and the stars and sun. Unlike any other city, there are trees and big flowers everywhere. It doesn't just sit in the middle of the jungle, baby. It's a part of it.

"The little people there are so nice, D. The parents are just a little shorter than you, and their kids are just a little taller. They get shorter as they grow up and level out when they get about my age. They're always happy. No one ever gets sick, and no one ever dies."

"What's it called Mama?" Deon asked. Love was so tired and in so much pain that she had almost not been able to talk any longer.

"It doesn't have a name, D. It's just a place we can meet at night when you go to sleep when I'm gone baby. Go brush your teeth sweetie. I'm hurting real bad right now and gotta try to go back to sleep," Love painfully said as a tear slid down the side of her cheek.

Deon slowly let go of his mother's hand and went into the bathroom to brush his teeth. Just as he started to walk away, Diondre woke up. Deon ran over and hugged him.

"She's real tired, daddy," he whispered just before he went into the bathroom. Diondre got up and stretched before leaning over to kiss his Love. She had quickly fallen asleep, but the pain she was in was still on her face. Mr. Riggs woke up next, and was simultaneously startled by Alexia.

"Thank God! You need to go to the doctor and get them to figure out why you snore so dang loud. You going to get us something to eat, Papa?"

Mr. Riggs couldn't help but laugh. He, Deon, and Diondre left to get breakfast for all of them a few moments later. Everyone engaged in conversation except for Deon. All he could think about is what his mother had told him that morning.

When they returned, Sarah and the doctor were in the room checking on Love. Mrs. Minnie and Alexia were quietly sitting on the couch. As Mr. Riggs and Mrs. Minnie prepared everyone's plate, Deon, Diondre, and Alexia watched as the doctor talked quietly to Sarah at the foot of Love's bed.

"Can I have a word with you guys really quickly?" the doctor asked Mrs. Minnie and Mr. Riggs as he walked towards them.

"Please sir, I need you to come along as well," he said as he looked at Diondre and continued towards the door.

"Y'all come on and eat." Mrs. Minnie said to Deon and Alexia as she made her way to the door following Mr. Riggs and Diondre.

Deon and Alexia ate quietly. Deon couldn't take his eyes off of his mother as she slept across the room. Alexia would glance over at Love, but she couldn't look at her for too long. She looked lifeless. They couldn't help but wonder about what the doctor needed to talk to everyone else about.

After a few minutes passed, Diondre, Mrs. Minnie, and Mr. Riggs came back into the room. The looks on their faces said it all. Diondre walked right pass the table and went into the bedroom. Mrs. Minnie's face was pinkish. It was more than obvious that she had just finished crying. Mr. Riggs had a serious look on his face. He sat down at the table and looked at both of the children before he spoke.

"After you finish eating, your grandmother wants you to pack your things," Mr. Riggs said as he began eating.

Alexia stared at Mr. Riggs for a moment before picking up her fork to begin eating again. Deon quietly excused himself from the table and went over to the foot of his mother's bed to look at her. Love was sleeping peacefully. Mrs. Minnie walked over towards Deon.

"Go pack your things baby. You're going home in a little while."

Deon immediately turned to hug Mrs. Minnie. There wasn't a need to say anything. The hurt in each of their hearts filled the room in that moment. They packed their things in silence. Diondre decided that it would be best for him to stay with Love.

As soon as they had finished packing, they went to Love's bed to say their goodbyes. Love was wide awake. Diondre sat in the chair next to her bed crying as he held her hand. Mrs. Minnie stood at the other side of Love's bed and stared out of the window.

Alexia approached the bed and leaned over to hug her mother. When she put her arms around her, Love closed her eyes and held on to her daughter as tightly as she could. It proved to be too much of an emotional moment for Mrs. Minnie. She rushed to the bathroom to keep from crying.

"I'm sorry, Mama," Alexia said as she quietly wept on Love's frail shoulder.

"I'm sorry baby. I love you," Love quietly responded. Her weakened voice made Alexia weep more and hold her tighter. After the elongated embrace, Alexia slowly pulled away and walked out of the room to Mr. Riggs' truck. As she walked down the hallway of the facility in tears, the nurses looked at her sympathetically. They had seen this scene too many times not to know what it meant.

Deon approached his teary-eyed mother slowly once Alexia walked out of the room. It was impossible for her not to smile when he came to her bed. He had a sad look on his face, but he didn't cry.

"I love you Mama," he said as he leaned over and embraced her.

"I love you too, D," Love said as she held him. While they embraced each other, Love had just

241

enough strength to tell him something that put a smile on his face before he stepped away.

"I'll see you tonight, baby." Deon's face suddenly brightened.

Mr. Riggs came over and softly grabbed Love's hand and told her that he would be back the following morning. In his heart, he was unsure if she would make it that long. He wanted her to fight to live just a little longer. He leaned down to kiss her on the forehead as he had done so many times before when she was a small girl. He grabbed the children's belongings and then made his way to the door. Just before Deon walked out with Mr. Riggs, he ran over and hugged his mother one more time and told her that he loved her. Love only had enough strength to smile.

When they got into the truck, Alexia was sitting there in tears texting one of her friends. Before they left, Mr. Riggs looked over at them both.

"It's all going to be just fine," he said.

They journeyed to Whiteville in almost complete silence. The sound of that old truck engine was the soundtrack of their long memorable ride home

# Chapter 8. A Promise Is A Promise

*God,*

*I know it's Your will Heavenly Father, but I need You to really, really comfort us right now while You take my baby, Lord. I don't know how much I can take right now, Lord. I've been raising these babies their whole lives and right when it seems like she got it all together, You take her, Father. I've never questioned You Lord and I never will, but I just ask that You comfort us right now. Comfort these babies Lord, and wrap Your arms around Diondre, Heavenly Father. He's taking it so bad Lord...*

Mrs. Minnie prayed as she paced back and forth in Love's living quarters. Sarah frequently stopped by the room throughout the day to make sure that she and the family were doing as well as they could be at a time such as this one. The pain had gotten so bad

243

that it couldn't be relieved with any medications. They opted to sedate her so that she wouldn't have to suffer. Diondre couldn't do anything but hold her hand. He only hoped that his presence still was able to comfort her.

Mrs. Minnie spent most of the day praying. Diondre would call for Mrs. Minnie every time that she would wake up. Neither one of them wanted to miss any of her last waking moments. Unfortunately, Love had become mute. The few minutes she stayed awake were spent looking at the ceiling. She didn't speak. She didn't move. She just stared.

Mrs. Minnie and Diondre were holding on to the little piece of Love that was left. Diondre could only stare at her lifeless frame while the last of her wilted away. However, Mrs. Minnie was at peace. God had answered her prayer. She would kiss Love throughout the day and place her hand on Diondre's shoulder for support and comfort. That only made him sadder. He realized more now than ever before that his true love would permanently leave his life.

Alexia cried herself to sleep that night in her room thinking of all the time she had spent hating her mother. She never allowed herself to see any of the good that dwelled within her. Mr. Riggs stayed up watching television in Mrs. Minnie's living room, while Deon sat beside him and wrote a letter to Bryce.

In the letter he detailed all the things that his mother had told him earlier. A majority of what he had written was a description of the place Love had told him about and how he would be able to meet her there each night that he went to sleep. It was the longest letter he had ever written to his brother. When he was finished, he sealed it in an envelope, stamped it, and rushed outside to place it in the mailbox. He wanted to make sure that it was there when the mailman came by the house the next morning. When he came back in the house, he hurried to ask his grandfather to tuck him in bed so that he could see the place that his mother had spoken so boldly of.

"Are you okay, D?" Mr. Riggs asked just before he turned out the light.

"I'm good. I'm just worried about Daddy and Grandma. I hope they're okay. I'm so tired." Deon let out an exaggerated yawn hoping that Mr. Riggs would exit the room to leave him to his thoughts. He had not told a soul about what his mother told him. Just as Deon had wished for, Mr. Riggs turned off the light and went downstairs to sleep on the couch.

Deon lay restless in his bed for what seemed like hours. He tossed and turned all night thinking about the place Love so vividly described. He figured that if he kept his eyes closed, sleep would eventually come. But it didn't. It only amplified the common sounds of the night. He could hear the cars passing on the street so clearly. The constant drip of the bathroom sink sounded like there was a metronome sitting on his nightstand. As irritating as it was, he counted each drop in hopes that it would help him fall asleep. And after a little over an hour, he did just that.

After a few hours passed, he slowly woke out of his deep sleep. A bright sunlight pierced through his eyelids forcing him to keep his eyes closed. In that instant he realized that he was not laying atop his soft bed. His little hands weren't touching the soft sheets he had grown accustomed to feeling each morning. They were pressing against soft, warm sand that was heated by the sun. When he finally opened his eyes, he found himself standing on the white sandy shore of what his mother had so vividly described.

He was standing right between the edge of a beautiful jungle and a mile tall wall of clear blue water that was only separated by forty yards of soft, white sand that warmed the soles of his feet as he slowly walked forward. He saw colorful fish and sea creatures that gracefully swam around as though he was not there.

The sight of the stars in the sky was just as his mother described. As captivating as all of the beautiful sights were, Deon's heart nearly stopped when he noticed a small group of swarthy mermaids with long-reddish hair swimming towards him. They were not typical mermaids. They had human like features from their shoulders to their wrists, but fins for hands that made them better suited to maneuver in their aquatic environment. The mermaids were at the wall's edge curiously gazing at him, and then they suddenly sped away. After they left, he looked at the wall around him and found that there were more mermaids than he had originally seen.

In an instant, he directed his attention to the jungle where he heard the rustling of leaves and the loud snapping of tree branches. Deon's feeling of astonishment suddenly turned into fear. He wasn't sure what was moving in the jungle, but he knew that it was moving quickly. There was nothing he could do but rush to the jungle's edge and crouch down under a plant whose leaves were as big as elephant ears.

Heavy snarling filled the air accompanied by the crescendo of jungle birds making noises as if they were warning everything in the jungle of an approaching threat. As Deon crouched under the large leaf, he closed his eyes tight and prayed fervently in silence. The louder the horrifying sounds became, the easier it was to determine that there was not just one creature. There was a herd.

A small hole in the leaf allowed Deon to take a quick glance towards the inside of the jungle. All he was able to see were falling branches and leaves. He realized that the herd was only a few hundred feet away from him. All of a sudden, there were multiple loud growls in the trees above his head followed by huge splashes of water. Deon saw a group of seven large beasts leaping from the jungle's edge into the wall of water.

The beasts all attacked a large whale-like sea creature and dragged it to the bottom. The other seas creatures quickly dispersed from the area in fear. As the beasts began to emerge from the wall of ocean with the large fish in their mouths, Deon could clearly see that they were actually lions. He tried his best to remain completely still and quiet, but he was afraid. He pressed his mouth against the leaf hoping that his heavy breathing would be drowned out by the noises of the jungle.

The beasts dragged the large fish through the sand close to the jungle's edge, and stopped only a few yards from the plant Deon was hiding under. They rested in silence around the animal as it flapped its large tail and fins. Deon tightly closed his eyes in fear that he would be eaten.

After a few minutes of silence, he decided to take a look at what was happening. To his amazement, he saw a small crowd of people surrounding the large fish and casually moving around the resting beasts without fear. They looked exactly as his mother had described.

There were short statured men and women of different races who wore white loose-fitting linen outfits. A small group of them were struggling to hold the fish's tail down while another small group of them carried a big needle with a dark liquid in it towards the underside of the creature. They slowly stuck the needle in, and almost immediately, it showed no more sign of life.

Seven of the small people mounted the backs of the lions and rode them back into the jungle. Deon carefully looked on from behind the tree trying with everything in him not to be noticed.

The entire group then gathered on the creature's underside and watched as one of the little men reached into the fish's birthing hole. Gasps filled the crowd as he pulled out a baby fish that was about the size of a small puppy. Cheers could be heard from everywhere as the little man hurried to the ocean wall and tossed the baby fish in it. Two of the black mermaids made their way to the small fish and carried it away deeper into the ocean as soon as it entered the water. After the cheers subsided, the group of little people rolled the large whale-like sea creature back into the ocean's wall.

Shortly after the large sea creature was back in the water, it regained consciousness and swam away into the ocean in the same direction the mermaids had taken its baby. A look of accomplishment filled their faces as they looked on. Just as Deon was moving

251

backward to completely hide himself behind the plant, a pleasant voice startled him.

"Who are you?" she said.

A girl, much taller than Deon, was standing right behind him a few feet away. He let out a loud scream and took off running as fast as he could. After a few strides, he tripped over a bundle of roots and bumped his head on the ground. He was unconscious.

When Deon woke up, the brightness of the sun made it hard for him to open his eyes just as it had done when he first woke up in that mysterious place. They had fitted him in a white linen outfit like theirs and laid him on a bed close to a glass wall in one of the buildings that overlooked the city. The light from the sun and stars reflected brightly off the adjacent buildings' windows.

As Deon looked around the large open-spaced room, he saw the strangest things. Eight feet high in the center of the room was a group of small fish that swam in a floating body of water the size of a twenty-gallon fish tank. The few paintings on the wall portrayed how they imagined the city would look at night. In each picture, the little people were staring at the moon. Bright-colored flowers grew along the high ceilings in full bloom. And the floor was made out of a soft, translucent material that felt amazing to walk on.

As soon as Deon got up from the bed in awe at what he had seen, three small people quickly walked in and stood before him. Their quick entrance made him somewhat petrified, but he couldn't let them know that he was scared. If they wanted to hurt him, they would have when he was unconscious.

"We were starting to wonder if you were going to sleep forever, but we figured from the way that you were farting that you would wake up sooner or later," one of them said as he walked a step closer to Deon.

"I don't know what's going on. First I was sleep, and then I woke up and was here. My mama told me about this place this morning," Deon replied.

"Where are you from boy?" asked the eldest of the three. Deon assumed that he was the eldest because of his wooden framed glasses, his wrinkled skin, and the slight hump in his back.

"I'm from Whiteville, North Carolina," Deon replied.

The three looked at each other puzzled. It was obvious they had never heard of Whiteville. The attention of everyone in the room shifted when the door opened. It was the girl who had discovered him on the edge of the jungle.

"Forgive our rudeness, young man. I'm Lo," the eldest of the group said as he extended his hand out to shake Deon's.

"This is my younger brother, Sterling," he said motioning his head to the younger looking slightly taller man to his right, "and this is my youngest brother Edward," he said as he motioned his head towards the even younger looking man to his right. Each of them shook Deon's hand.

"I'm Neesah. Lo's daughter," the young girl said as she made her way over to Deon with her hand extended. She was only a few inches taller than Deon, but he assumed that she was much older because of her height.

Her hair was much like that of Love's, but longer. She wore it in one long ponytail that stopped at her waist.

"I'm Deon. My mom told me to meet her here this morning."

The three little men looked a little confused as they stood before him. It was the second time that Deon made mention of his mother and they had no clue as to why the young man's mother had knowledge of the place, or why she would tell the young man to meet her there.

"When is she supposed to meet you here, boy?" Sterling curiously asked.

"I don't know exactly when, but it'll be soon," Deon replied.

"Well we'll have a big welcome party for her since we know she's coming," Sterling said excitingly.

"We rarely get visitors here. Maybe once every few hundred years or so. Neesah will show you around and we'll prepare a celebration like you've never dreamed of." A joyous spirit filled the room.

Neesah grabbed Deon by the hand and quickly led him out of the room as the three little men followed. They hurried to an elevator that was at the end of a long empty hallway. Once Deon and Neesah got on the elevator, the three men stopped walking. While Deon and Neesah were being whisked down to the bottom floor, Lo began fussing at other little men for the mess that they had just created.

"Sterling, why do you always have to open that big mouth of yours before that tiny little brain in your head thinks about what you say?" Lo asked.

"You don't have a clue about who this boy is! And now you got him thinking that we're having a celebration for his mama. We don't even know who she is, or anything!" Edward said.

"Well I'm sorry. What was I supposed to do? He looked like he was going to jump out of his skin when he saw us," Sterling replied.

256

"Let's just go to Priest Lance. He'll know what's going on," Lo said.

Priest Lance was the wisest man in that place. He was also the chief clergyman. If anyone knew why Deon was there, it would be him. The three hurried to see him.

When Deon and Neesah stepped out of the elevator, Neesah grabbed his hand and quickly ran through the beautiful lobby of the building. The area was elegantly furnished in all white. Each wall was constructed of tinted glass and a tall ceiling very similar to that which was in the room he had just left out of moments ago. The room was filled with bright blooming flowers and columns of water that connected the ceiling to the floor. Deon couldn't stop to admire anything because Neesah was dragging him along swiftly.

"There's so much to show you," Neesah said.

As they got closer to the front door, Deon saw things that he could never even imagine. There were tons of little people on the streets. Some of them were riding on the backs of large lions, while others rode on the backs of tapirs. There were also groups of people who taxied on top of elephants that walked along the sidewalks. All of the beasts seemed to be well tamed aside from the occasional sounds of the wild they called out.

There were a few amongst the people that were just as tall as Neesah. It was weird to see that the children were taller than the adults.

Neesah hurried Deon through the crowds talking as fast as she could, but he was much too fascinated by everything he was seeing to listen. The mix of the jungle and urban culture was interesting to say the least. Neesah's voice was reduced to a mere murmur to him.

"I have to take you to Mt. Olive, Deon. From there, we'll be able to look down and see everything," Neesah said as she quickly maneuvered through the crowd holding tight to Deon's hand. As they went along, the little people stared at Deon and whispered amongst themselves. They were just as fascinated by him as he was of them.

After a few blocks of walking, Neesah walked Deon down one of the side streets that led directly out of the city into the jungle. One of the large lions was resting under a tree that sat on the side of the street. As they approached, it quickly rose to its feet and vigorously ran towards them. Deon immediately squeezed Neesah's hand and tried to run the other way.

"What's wrong with you, boy?" she said as she yanked her hand away from him. All Deon could see was the huge feline running towards them as he looked at the unmoved girl.

"Don't worry. He's coming to give us a ride. There's absolutely nothing to be afraid of here, Deon. Absolutely nothing."

When the lion made it to them, Neesah quickly hoisted herself on its strong back and extended her hand to Deon. Deon hesitantly climbed up and held on tight around Neesah's waist. She chuckled as the lion took off for the jungle. As soon as they entered, the beast climbed to the top of the trees and leaped from one branch to another. After a few miles of travel, Deon was no longer afraid.

It took them roughly fifteen minutes to reach a clearing in the jungle. There was an enormous hill that bordered the ocean wall and overlooked the entire place. When they reached the top and dismounted, the large lion walked over to the ocean wall and drank from it before lying down to rest.

"This is the highest point here, Deon. We can see everything from up here," Neesah said as she and Deon marveled at the glorious sight overlooking everything.

The tops of tall buildings in the distance emerged from the jungle. Some of the trees were as tall as the highest buildings and there were manicured vines that crawled up each wall. Mountains were far in the distance and clues of small communities surrounding the city could be seen in patches where the jungle was thin. The wall of ocean that surrounded everything disappeared behind the distant mountains. The sound of ocean was constant and faint, and the smell reminded Deon of Myrtle Beach.

Neesah pointed out all the wonders from the mount. She told him how things were and how things had always been. They knew no pain or sickness, and death never came. People grew shorter and older, but after sixty-years-old they stopped counting the years and physically remained the same.

As they talked on top of the mount Deon shared what it was like in Whiteville, North Carolina. Neesah was overly fascinated by the things that Deon thought were very much normal. The idea of television made Neesah's eyes glow.

After a while they hopped back onto the back of the lion and rode down to where they saw children playing beside the wall of ocean. Tall children played and swam in the ocean. Some of the adults walked along the sand and rested on the edge. Animals of every kind harmoniously lived amongst them. As they walked, Deon noticed that a few of the older people were on their knees in a posture of prayer.

"What are they doing?" he asked as they passed by a couple kneeling in the sand.

"They're praying, Deon. What does it look like they're doing?" Neesah replied as she chuckled.

"So, you all believe in God?" Deon asked.

"Doesn't everyone?"

Deon didn't respond. He was too busy taking in all the glory of that place. As badly as Neesah wanted to ask Deon more questions about his mother, she didn't. Something in her heart was telling her not to.

The three elders had made their way out of the city to Priest Lance's dwelling. He lived in a beautiful chapel in one of the small jungle communities about twenty miles from the heart of the city. When they arrived Priest Lance was outside of the chapel feeding the lions fresh vegetables from the huge garden behind the chapel.

"I was wondering what was taking you old geezers so long," he said waving at the three of them as they got off the huge elephant.

Priest Lance was a fit, dark skinned man who grew a pure white beard and had a completely bald head. They all went inside the chapel and the three quickly began telling him of the young boy who mysteriously showed up. As they had already known, Priest Lance knew Deon was there.

"The boy's mother is going on to be with Jesus, but there's something we have to help him with. I knew this was coming. I just didn't think it would be so soon," he said as he paced the middle isle of the chapel.

"What exactly is it that we're supposed to be helping him with?" Sterling sincerely asked.

"The effectual prayer of a righteous man availeth much, Sterling," he quickly replied.     "That boy's family has sent more prayers up to Heaven than most. But God spoke to me a few days ago about one in particular. One that caused a group of angels to cry with tears of joy."

Priest Lance was referring to Love's last prayer with her entire family in her quarters. Of all the prayers she had prayed throughout her life, that one was from the deepest depths of her soul.

"Go get the boy and bring him back here," Priest Lance said.

"But what about the celebration for his mom?" Sterling blurted. Lo and Edward cringed as soon as those words left his lips. They knew that they'd messed up by telling Deon that they were throwing a welcoming party for Love.

"Please tell me that you don't have that child thinking that his mother is coming here!!!" Priest Lance screamed. They all immediately put their heads down in shame.

"Well, we didn't know what to do. He was so excited and all about meeting his mom here. It only seemed right that we did something special...We didn't know," Edward said.

"Just go get the boy, please," Priest Lance replied.

The three men rushed out of the chapel and went to find Deon and Neesah. Priest Lance sat on the front pew of the chapel and prayed.

When the three men made it back to the heart of the city a large crowd had gathered in a park not far from the building Deon had awaken in. Loud cheering and music filled the air. From the top of the elephant they could see that the people were serenading Deon with song and dance as he and Neesah sat on a low limb of a tree towards the center of the park. The three men struggled through the crowd to get to them. The music abruptly stopped when they cut right in the middle of the group that was dancing in front of the tree.

"Deon, come down quickly boy. We have to take you to see the priest right away," Edward shouted up to Deon. He and Neesah hurried down and quickly followed the three men back to the large elephant that had carried them.

As soon as they all climbed on top of the large beast someone from the crowd shouted towards them.

"We'll start preparing for your mom's celebration right away!" The three men just looked at each other as the elephant sped off back to the chapel. Deon's mouth was moving a mile-a-minute telling the three men about all the places and things that Neesah had showed him.

When they arrived, Priest Lance was standing on the steps of the chapel rubbing the mane of one of the largest lions that Deon had seen in his life. As they got off the elephant, the lion quickly ran towards Deon. It sniffed him from head to toe and then ran back over to Priest Lance. It let out a roar that could be heard for miles and then rested beside the Priest.

"Welcome Deon. I hope you've been enjoying your stay. Come with me. We have a lot to talk about."

Deon and Priest Lance went inside the chapel with the small group following close behind. Deon was surprised at how much the chapel looked like all the churches he had been in before with his grandmother. He was shocked to see a large portrait of Jesus' crucifixion on the back wall of the chapel. He led them all to the dining area and sat them down at the table.

"Deon, a few days ago God spoke to me while I was praying. He told me all about you. I knew you were coming. I just really had no clue that you were going to visit us so soon young man. Will the rest of you please excuse Deon and I? We need a moment alone. I could really use some help cleaning the sanctuary, if you all don't mind." The others filed out of the room and back

266

into the sanctuary. It was as clean as it always was, but they knew Priest Lance needed to be alone with Deon. They sat and listened to Neesah tell them about the time she spent with him and what she had learned about him. In the dining room, Priest Lance poured them both a glass of tea as they sat.

"Deon, things are very different here but there's one thing that'll remain the same wherever there's a living thing. God is God. You can travel a gazillion miles either way you want to from the sun, and God will be the same God there that He is anywhere. It's the absolute truth."

"Is this Heaven?"

"Absolutely not, boy! There's not a place in any galaxy that exist that can even come close to being Heaven, Deon. I know you've seen a lot of things today, but none of this can compare to the glory of Heaven."

"Then what is this place?"

"Well, it's exactly what your mother told you Deon. There's no such thing as time here. Night

267

never comes so it's just been one long day for us for as long as I can remember. We start out as tall as Neesah and get shorter as we age. It is much different than what you're accustomed to Deon. Too much to explain. Simply put, we're just a place between you and Heaven," Priest Lance answered. Deon looked very confused.

"When is my mom coming?" Deon asked. As Priest Lance began to answer Deon suddenly began to get extremely drowsy. His vision blurred and Priest Lance rushed to his side to keep him from falling out of his chair.

"Deon, you're about to wake up son. It's very important that you tell your papa to give Mrs. Minnie the note."

"What note?"

"Just make sure you tell him to give it to her Deon. We'll see you when you get back young boy," Priest Lance replied as he struggled to hold Deon upright in the chair. That was the last thing the young boy remembered before he woke up in the comfort of his own bed at Mrs. Minnie's house.

Deon couldn't believe what had just happened. He sprang from his bed, and ran to the door.

"Alexia!" he screamed as he ran across the hall to his sister's room. The morning sun hit his face as soon as he opened the door. When he didn't see her, he ran downstairs calling for her and his grandfather.

"We're down here," Mr. Riggs screamed back.

When Deon reached the bottom of the stairs he saw that Mrs. Minnie, Mr. Riggs, Alexia, and Mr. Harry Lennon's parents were all sitting quietly in the living room. His excitement ceased instantly when he saw the sadness on their faces. In that moment, Deon knew that his mother was gone.

Mrs. Minnie got up and walked over to Deon with a face full of tears. She knelt down and hugged him as he stood motionless in front of her.

"Your mother passed away early this morning, baby," Mrs. Minnie softly said to him. Those words pierced his heart. This time it was impossible for the young boy to be as strong as he had been before. He cried uncontrollably in his grandmother's arms.

"It'll be okay baby. She's not going to hurt anymore, baby."

Deon instinctively walked over to his sister who sat on the couch crying. She leaned forward to embrace him and assured him that everything would get better. Mr. Riggs and Mr. Harry Lennon's parents walked over to console them both. Mrs. Minnie excused herself to her room and closed the door. The weight of emotions was far too much for her to bear.

She paced back and forth praying that God would comfort them. What started as soft, intense prayer, quickly turned into loud, passionate pleading. She was begging God to remove their pain. The thunderous prayer seemed to shake the inner walls of the house.

"Where's my dad?" Deon asked as the rest of the family stood in the living room.

"He wasn't doing too well, D. Your grandmother dropped him off at home on their way here," Mr. Riggs replied.

Alexia and Deon went back upstairs. Mr. Harry Lennon's father started to follow the children, but Mr.

Riggs motioned for him to stay in the living room so that they could each spend time alone. Before Deon got to his room, he remembered what he was supposed to tell his grandfather. He rushed back downstairs so that he could whisper in his ear.

"Give Grandma the note." Mr. Riggs' face was filled with confusion. He had no earthly idea what he was talking about.

"What note, D?" Mr. Riggs softly asked.

"I don't know Papa. They just told me to tell you

Mr. Riggs was left dumbfounded in his chair. He had too much on his mind to even begin to think about what Deon had told him. He went to Mrs. Minnie's room to see if she was doing any better. There were no sounds coming from her room, so he knew she had finished praying. When he entered, he found his beautiful daughter sitting on the edge of her bed.

"Daddy, I sat right there and saw my baby take her last breath. I always thought she was goin' to be the one burying me."

Mr. Riggs closed the door behind him and walked over and put his hand on Mrs. Minnie's shoulder.

"It's all going to be alright, sweetie. God knows exactly what he's doing. You just have to trust him. She ain't gotta hurt no more, Minnie." He sat down beside her and held her in his arms. It always had seemed to make Mrs. Minnie feel better when she was a little girl, but it did not have the same effect that day.

"I could have tried harder when she got out there, Daddy. Even when she was all the way gone I could have at least spent more time with her. These folks think I killed Harry. Now my baby gone and all I can think about is all the time I could have spent with her while she was here. These babies ain't got nobody but us and they good-for-nothing daddy."

"Minnie them babies are going to be fine, and you're going to be just fine too. You know you did all you could have done. This is just what happens in life baby. It's life. Lie down and get you some rest sweetie. I'm going to go check on the kids and see about letting Bryce know. Get some rest baby. I love you."

As Mr. Riggs walked back into the living room, Mr. Harry Lennon's parents bid their goodbyes for the day and left. After seeing them out, Mr. Riggs made his way up the stairs. He could hear Alexia's music playing through her cracked room door. He peered in and saw that she was laying in her bed texting someone.

"You okay Lexy?" he asked. She nodded and continued texting.

It was absolutely quiet in Deon's room and the door was closed. Mr. Riggs lightly knocked on the door before opening it. When he entered, Deon was lying on his bed writing. Mr. Riggs came in and quietly sat on his bed.

"You writing Bryce?"

"Yea."

"What were you talking about earlier Deon? You said something about giving Grandma a note."

"Did you give it to her?!?"

"D, I have no idea what kind of note you're talking about."

273

Deon looked at him without saying a word for a moment before turning over to continue writing. Mr. Riggs stood up and walked over to the window to peer out at the morning sun.

"How are you feeling, D?" Mr. Riggs asked.

"It hurts Papa, but we all knew it was coming so I guess it's not as bad," Deon replied as he continued writing his letter to Bryce lying across his bed.

Thoughts of Love ran through Mr. Riggs' mind as he stared out the window. There were many memories that flashed in his head in a short period of time. When Love came into the world, she taught him the most valuable lesson he had ever learned. She made him realize that it was easier to love than to not ever love at all. In the midst of his grief, he smiled knowing that without her he would have disliked black people for the rest of his life with no reason at all.

"Papa, I'm worried about my dad," Deon said, looking back at him as he folded his letter and placed it in an envelope.

"He'll be fine, D. It's going to be real tough for him for a while, but he'll be just fine. I'll stop by there and check on him."

Mr. Riggs walked over and gave him a hug before leaving the room.

"I'll be back a little later. Make sure your Grandma gets some rest," he said as he walked out the door, closing it behind him.

Mr. Riggs checked in on Alexia and Mrs. Minnie before he left. Both of them were napping. It had been a rough day for everyone. He got into his old truck and drove straight to Love's apartment. As he pulled into the housing project, people on both sides of the street waved and smiled at him. He figured that most of them had found out about Love's passing. Everyone in that community loved her. When he knocked on the door, Diondre did not answer. He knocked a few more times before he decided to leave. Just as he was stepping back into his truck, one of the residents walked up to the window.

"He left out walking about an hour ago. Sorry about Love. Everybody loved her round here."

"Thank you for letting me know."

Mr. Riggs pulled off and rode all through town looking for Diondre. He couldn't be found anywhere. He even tried calling his cell phone a few times with no luck. After an hour had passed, he went home and contacted the prison so they could inform Bryce that his mother had passed. After he made the call, he went to his closet and pulled out an old photo album that he had tucked away years ago. It was filled with pictures that he had collected through the years. There were a lot of pictures of him and Mrs. Minnie's mother. Of course, he had pictures of all of his grandchildren. He spent over an hour looking through his album. Each photo brought back sweet memories. He looked at those photographs until he fell asleep.

Meanwhile at the prison, Mr. Coot was reading his Bible aloud for Bryce. He was reading the story of Job, which told of how he had kept his faith through all of the tests and trials God allowed him to go through. Suddenly, they were approached by the guards who were instructed to take Bryce to the warden's office. When he entered, the chaplain and warden were sitting there waiting for him. Bryce began to cry as soon as he saw the chaplain. He knew that his mother had passed away.

"Is it my mother?" Bryce softly asked as he stood in the doorway.

"She passed earlier this morning," the chaplain regretfully replied.

Bryce fell to his knees and began to weep right there in the doorway. They didn't know what to say. They knew that Bryce had always been a responsible young man who never caused any trouble. The warden felt horribly. He had heard the story behind why Bryce was in prison. The counselor had come into his office many times and discussed Bryce with him.

"Okay," Bryce simply said after a few moments. He stood up and turned around so that the guards could escort him back to his cell.

"Bryce, we're going to make arrangements so that you can go to the funeral," the chaplain said as Bryce turned around to be escorted away. He nodded his head to show his gratitude. When he returned to his cell, Coot was still reading the Bible. When he saw the sadness on Bryce's face, he took off his glasses, and walked over to put his hand on Bryce's shoulder.

"Is it your mom?" he asked.

Bryce nodded his head. Tears immediately began flowing as the guards closed the cell bars behind him. Mr. Coot prayed for the young man as they stood there. He begged God to give Bryce the strength to make it through this trying time in his life. The longer he prayed, the more the tears flowed from his eyes. For the rest of the day, Bryce spent time talking to Mr. Coot about the times that he shared with his mother.

Back at Mrs. Minnie's house, Deon tried his best to go to sleep. He desperately wanted to go back to that place that he dreamed of the night before. When Mrs. Minnie walked upstairs to check on the children, she found Alexia listening to her music and Deon playing his

278

video games. Unfortunately for Deon, his napping throughout the day did not result in the dream he had hoped for. Each time he woke up and realized that he was in his bed, he was disappointed.

"But you promised," he softly said to himself as he woke up from one of his naps. He was referring to the promise his mother made about him always being able to visit her there after she died. Deon stayed in his room for the remainder of the day, only coming downstairs to eat some of the pizza Mrs. Minnie had ordered for them.

Mr. Riggs came to the house just as the pizza delivery man arrived. On his way to the door, he paid and tipped him before he made it to the porch of the house. Alexia and Deon came downstairs to sit at the kitchen table. Mr. Riggs made sure that he stayed upbeat and told funny stories in an attempt to keep everyone smiling.

"Deon, when your mom was about your age I noticed she would never eat corn. That thing bothered me so bad. One day we were all sitting right here eating and your granddaddy was getting on her about eating her vegetables, as he always did. Just as soon as your grandparents walked out the room for a second and she thought I wasn't looking, she raked that corn right off the plate and put it in a napkin and stuffed it right in her pocket." He was laughing the entire time he was telling the story.

"When she realized I caught her, she got up and begged me not to tell them. That little girl told me that the reason she didn't eat corn was because she could see every kernel come out when she went to the bathroom after she ate it. I laughed so hard your grandparents came running back in. She just sat there and acted like nothing happened. I promised her I wouldn't say nothing."

"That's why my dag gone corn kept getting missing out the pantry!" Mrs. Minnie said as they all laughed.

"Yeah, she was mess," Mr. Riggs replied.

After they finished eating their pizza, Deon and Alexia went up to their rooms to get dressed for bed. On Deon's way upstairs, he thought hard about the promise his mother made to him. Sleep didn't come easy for Deon or Alexia that night. Alexia spent the rest of her evening talking to her on the phone with her friends until she eventually fell asleep. The naps that Deon had taken throughout the day made it extremely difficult for him to sleep. He stared at the ceiling concentrating on the place between there and Heaven until he finally dozed off.

# Chapter 9. "...For The Good Of Those Who Love Him"

Deon sluggishly woke up in the same bed of the building that he woke up in before. This time, Neesah and the three old men were sitting on the side of his bed smiling at him.

"Is my mom here?" Deon asked as he sat up on the large bed. Sterling was the first to speak.

"Not yet, Deon. But when she does get here, we have a celebration prepared for her that's going to top any party you've ever witnessed!"

"Did he give the note to your grandmother, Deon?" Lo sternly asked.

"I told him to, but he didn't know what I was talking about." Neesah hugged Deon in excitement as soon as he stood.

"Deon, you've got to see everything we've done. I'll show you. Come on." She grabbed Deon's hand and quickly turned to head downstairs to show him.

"Hold up you two. We can see it all on the way back from the chapel to see Priest Lance. He's instructed us to bring you back there as soon as you returned" Edward said.

Neesah and Deon were immediately stopped in their tracks. The three old men led the way down the hall to the elevator that took them down to the first floor. When they made through the lobby and out the front door, there was an elephant waiting to take them back to the chapel.

When they walked out of the front door of the building, Deon was in total awe of what he saw. People were running around the city hastily decorating the streets for Love's celebration. They had draped the forest canopy above the streets with an assortment of beautiful sheer cloths. Each side of the street was lined with a glittery material that shimmered in the light. Hundreds of large fluorescent birds hovered beneath the forest canopy singing the most beautiful tune in unison as they flew in an orchestrated pattern that was directed by an older little man who stood in the middle of the street as others moved around him hurrying about their separate duties. The smell of baked breads along with other fresh scents that Deon had never smelled before filled the air.

As they mounted the elephant and hurried to the chapel, Deon saw separate groups of little people rehearsing a dance and decorating different parts of the city with colorful flowers. Animals of all sorts were assisting them as they prepared.

"All this for my mom?" Deon asked as he held on tightly to Neesah as the elephant hurried the group to the chapel.

"I told you," Lo replied as they made their journey.

While Deon enjoyed the company of his new found friends, Mr. Riggs and Mrs. Minnie sat in her living room coping with the lost of Love without saying a word. They sat on the couch both wondering how long it would be before they would become emotionally stable again.

"Daddy, what did I do so wrong? First Mama, then Harry, and now my baby."

"Minnie, you can't take the credit or blame yourself for God's doing. Baby, when that sun rises every morning, you don't sit back and admire your glory. It's His. And you can't say it's your fault, or that anything is even wrong when He calls one of His angels back home, baby. Matter fact…" He paused and reached into one of his front pockets, pulling out a folded sheet of paper. He held his head down as he held on to it as if it was the most important thing he had ever held in his life.

"What's wrong daddy?"

"I wasn't ever supposed to let you see this. If I would have had the slightest idea that you would go on all these years blaming yourself, I would have showed you a long time ago."

Mr. Riggs reluctantly gave Mrs. Minnie the folded sheet. As soon as he placed it in her hand, he got up off the couch and walked over to the window to stare at the moon. As Mrs. Minnie began reading, she realized that it was the note that her mother left Mr. Riggs before committing suicide.

"It took me decades to stop blaming myself Minnie. It wasn't the fact that I didn't forgive her for what she did. It was the fact that I didn't forgive myself for neglecting her all those years. If I would have just stayed out of those bars and spent more time with her. If I would have just stayed off of that bottle and away from them damn women...Minnie, I knew my workers weren't looking at you and her no type of way. She just wanted my attention, and she was crying out for me to give it to her. That's why she cheated. If I would have been a man and forgiven myself and loved her for all the time I didn't, she'd probably be right here right now, baby. You weren't the reason she put that bullet in her head."

Shock overtook Mrs. Minnie as she read the note. She would have never guessed that her mother cheated. At the same time, a great burden was lifted off of her. For a majority of her life, she believed that she was the reason why her mother ended her life so tragically.

"Daddy, it was her own personal choice. You can't blame you for her making that decision, and I stopped kicking myself years ago for thinking it was because of me and Harry. At least I thought I did. But you gotta preach to your own choir. You can't go on blaming you, for life."

Mrs. Minnie got up off the couch and walked over to comfort her father. They wept together in front of the window as Mr. Riggs laid his head on her shoulder. For the first time ever, Mrs. Minnie had to be strong for her father. When their tears ended, they both prayed for a better tomorrow and fell asleep.

When Deon, Neesah, and the three old men made it to the chapel, they hurried inside. Priest Lance was kneeling in front of the alter praying when they entered. They quietly sat down in the pews a few rows from the front. Priest Lance knew they were there, but he didn't cease praying. They sat quietly and waited for him to turn to acknowledge their presence.

287

"Welcome back young man. Thank you for delivering the message to your papa," Priest Lance said happily.

"Why did you tell me to tell him to give my grandma a note? He didn't know what I was talking about."

"Why so many questions Deon? Just know that it will help answer one of your mom's most important prayers."

"When is she going to get here?" Deon asked as he quickly rose from his seat and walked down the aisle towards him. Priest Lance's face was immediately filled with frustration. He knew that Sterling, Lo, and Edward had not yet told Deon the truth.

"Sterling! Lo! Edward! I need to speak with you in private, right now! Deon, give us a second please."

The three men quickly followed Priest Lance out of the chapel with their heads bowed in shame. They knew that they had made a terrible mistake. As soon as they made it outside, Priest Lance slammed the door of the chapel behind them. The loud noise echoed throughout the chapel's walls.

"What were we supposed to do, Sir? By the time we got back to the city everyone was already preparing for a celebration," Sterling replied.

"Priest Lance, we got caught up and excited. Before we knew it, he popped up again," Edward said.

"You three have no idea how devastated that young man is going to be when he figures out that you've lied to him. There's no time to deal with this right now. He's got to go back," Priest Lance said as he paced back and forth.

"He just got here," Lo said.

Priest Lance quickly ran back into the chapel as the three old men followed close behind. Deon and Neesah were laughing in the chapel until they saw them hurrying back towards them.

"Come with me, quickly," Priest Lance said as passed by Deon and Neesah and headed to the back of the chapel. Deon hurried behind him. Priest Lance led him to a small living room near the dining area.

"Sit down dear boy. The rest of you can wait in the dining room. I'll deal with all of you shortly." Priest Lance directed Deon to take a seat on one of the couches. He sat down eagerly awaiting Priest Lance's next words.

Priest Lance reached into one of his pockets and pulled out a small glowing vile of liquid. He raised it up above his head and carefully examined it.

"What is that?" Deon curiously asked.

"This, my friend, is going to help you go to sleep."

"What in the world do you want me to go to sleep for!? I've been sleep all day!"

"Deon, we have about five of your minutes to get you home. You've gotta do something extremely important. I wish there was enough time to explain, but you've gotta get home and get in contact with your dad before it's too late."

"My Dad? What's wrong with him?"

"Nothing is wrong with him. But if you don't hurry up and get this message to him, it's going to be bad Deon. Please. You have to drink this now."

Deon stared at the glowing liquid in the vile for a short moment, and then hesitantly took it from him to drink. It took effect almost immediately. His eyelids grew heavy as he slumped back in the couch and dropped the vile on the ground. Priest Lance quickly helped Deon get in a more comfortable position.

"Deon, you have to call your dad right away and tell him not to knock on the red door." Deon had just enough energy to slightly nod his head to let him know that he understood. Priest Lance placed his hand on Deon's head and began praying as he drifted into a deep sleep. That was the last thing Deon remembered before waking up in his room.

When he opened his eyes, he heard the sound of rain pounding against his bedroom window followed by the flashes of lightning and roars of thunder. The only thing that he could focus on was what Priest Lance had instructed him to do. The young man quickly sprang out of his bed and darted down the hallway to Bryce's old room. It was the only room upstairs that had a landline.

291

He sat on Bryce's bed and called his father's cell phone. After a few rings, Diondre answered the phone.

"Daddy, don't knock on the red door!" Deon whispered.

"What? Deon, what in the hell are you doing up this late boy? It's almost three in the morning! You ok son?" Diondre was slurring every word. He had used enough cocaine and drank enough beer to numb the pain of losing Love temporarily.

"I'm fine daddy. Just please don't knock on the red door. I gotta go before someone hears me up. I love you."

Deon quickly hung up the phone and hurried back down the hallway into his bedroom. He jumped back in his bed and lay there thinking of why Priest Lance told him to deliver yet another urgent message to one of his family members. None of it made sense to him.

As for Diondre, he stood in the rain looking at his phone in confusion. When Deon called him, he had gotten caught in the storm while walking through the town. That day he had gone from one bar to the other to drink and used every drug that he could get his hands on. Although

292

he didn't have any money, everyone gave him what he needed to help him deal with the passing of his first and only true love. He was extremely drunk when Deon called. When his phone rang, he had just begun walking up to a drug dealer's house. He knew the dealer would give him cocaine on credit because of what happened to Love. As he made his way to the house, he thought about Love and the red door that Deon had just told him about.

As he stumbled up the driveway murmuring incomprehensibly, he looked up and was almost stunned sober. He fell to his knees in the middle of the driveway petrified at what stood before him. The light on the front porch was just bright enough to show a red door at the entrance of the house.

His phone slowly slipped out of his hand and onto the ground. The broken man wept hysterically with the weight of his body pressing down on the asphalt beneath him. The rain beat against his back as the earth shook beneath him. He stayed in that posture thinking about how his children needed him more than they ever had before. When he held Love's hand as she took her last breath, he promised her that he would better himself for her and the children. After all the promises he had made to her, this was the one that Love wouldn't be able to forgive him for if he had broken it.

He got up off the ground and walked away. He no longer desired to drink. He no longer desired to use cocaine. His commitment to his promise to Love was the only thing on his mind at that moment. As he walked away, he saw the lights of a car quickly turning into the driveway he had just left. He didn't turn back around to see who it was. Deon's message had been enough for him to keep focused. Not long after, a hail of gunshots startled Diondre. In his drunken state, he ran as quickly as he could in the opposite direction. He didn't stop until he had almost reached Love's apartment in the projects. He stopped at the corner and vomited everything that he had eaten that day. Soaked and exhausted, he walked inside and cried himself to sleep.

When the sun rose the next morning, the heavy rain still had not ceased. Mrs. Minnie rose early as she always did. Before preparing breakfast, she fixed Mr. Riggs a cup of coffee. The smell of it brewing in the kitchen woke him up. When she brought it to him, he sat up and turned the television to the morning news.

"Good morning, Daddy."

"Good morning, Beautiful. Look at this."

In the early hours of the morning, a home invasion took place at a local residence known for being a crack house. Three people were fatally wounded. Based on the evidence collected, the authorities believed that it was a robbery. However, when crimes like that took place in the community, there were hardly ever any witnesses.

Mrs. Minnie and Mr. Riggs were in shock. Things like that rarely happened in Whiteville. When Mrs. Minnie was finished preparing breakfast, Mr. Riggs called Deon and Alexia downstairs to eat. Deon came running down first, with Alexia following soon after. The storm had put everyone in a gloomy mood that morning.

After they prayed, they ate and talked amongst themselves. Deon was quiet for the most part. Mr. Riggs couldn't take his eyes off of his grandson. He still couldn't figure out what made him mention that note, but he was elated to finally have a burdened lifted off of his heart.

That day Mrs. Minnie and Alexia had many things to do in preparation of Love's burial. Deon and Mr. Riggs left so that they could begin to move everything out of Love's apartment. When they arrived, Diondre was sitting on the couch watching television. The sight of Deon made him run over to hug his son like he never hugged him before.

"Are you ok?" Deon asked as Diondre held him tight.

"I'm good son. I love you."

"Diondre, we are going to start boxing up everything and moving it over to my house. You can take whatever you want. I just want to get it done. It shouldn't take us too long."

The three left to rent a U-Haul truck and pick up some boxes to move everything. As they moved the belongings out of the house, Diondre and Deon communicated with each other in a way that they had never done before. One of Diondre's friends helped them move out the larger things so that they could be done by that evening. The rain did not subside until late that afternoon, so they were very grateful for the help. Before it had gotten dark, the three of them had completely emptied Love's apartment and moved everything into Mr. Riggs' home.

"Diondre, you and D can go ahead and take the U-Haul back and pick up the truck. Be careful out there on that wet road. I gotta put a set of tires on the front of that thing."

The two returned the U-Haul and hopped in Mr. Riggs truck to head back to Mr. Riggs' house. On the way back, Diondre couldn't hold his tongue any longer. He had to know how his son knew about the red door.

"D, how did you know where I was at last night son?"

"I don't know where you where at last night."

"C'mon Deon, what made you call me..."

Before Diondre could finish, the steering wheel of that old truck started to vibrate. Simultaneously, the rear of the truck slightly fishtailed from one side to the other. The combination of the wet roads with two bad tires caused the truck to hydroplane. To make matters worse, they were just about to cross the bridge in town that flooded every time that it rained.

"Daddy!" Deon screamed.

"Hold on!" Diondre screamed back frantically as he tried to regain control of the truck.

Diondre instinctively slammed on brakes and jerked the wheel to keep the truck from going into the river that flowed beneath the bridge. That was the worst thing he could have done. The truck ran off of the road right before they reached the guardrail. The driver's side of the truck bed slammed into the guardrail causing the truck to flip upside down and land into the flooded river. Both of them were knocked unconscious from the impact of the truck slamming against the water.

Diondre quickly regained consciousness. The truck was upside down and completely submerged in the water, and the darkness made it almost impossible to see anything. With one hand, Diondre struggled to unfasten his seatbelt. As soon as he was free to move, he reached over to unfasten Deon's seatbelt too. Deon looked completely lifeless. Diondre pulled Deon up to the surface and swam to the riverbank with his son's limp body. Luckily, witnesses nearby had called for an ambulance.

As soon as they were both out of the water, Diondre began CPR. Blood gushed profusely from a large gash in his head. He was severely wounded and felt faint, but his adrenaline wouldn't allow him to stop trying to revive his son. He continuously breathed into Deon's mouth and pumped his chest. Nothing happened. Soon, Diondre heard the sound of sirens and saw bright red flashing lights.

Diondre gathered the strength to pick Deon up to take him to the ambulance. The paramedics quickly grabbed Deon and helped Diondre into the ambulance so they could leave for the hospital that was located two miles away from their accident. Onlookers watched in horror worried about what would happen to them.

"Sir, I need you to stay calm. We're almost at the hospital okay? You'll be fine," the paramedic said.

"Please God, don't take my baby," Diondre said. The loss of blood was making him weaker with every passing moment. He fell in and out of consciousness as they rode straight to the emergency room.

Deon's body lay in the back of the ambulance, but his mind had drifted to his favorite place. He woke up on the sand bordering the ocean wall. When he completely opened his eyes, he saw that he was surrounded by dozens of small people. Each one of them looked sad. Deon was puzzled. They had always been so happy to see him each time he came. Furthermore, he couldn't understand why he had not awakened in the bed that he had awakened in each time before.

Neesah, Lo, Sterling, Edward, and Priest Lance stood by his feet and moved closer to him as he lifted himself off the ground to sit up. He was exhausted and completely drenched.

"What's wrong? Why are all of you looking so sad?"

"Deon, I'm sorry to disappoint you. But we can't go on allowing you to believe that..." Just as Priest Lance was about to finish his sentence, the ground around them started to tremble and lions began to roar ferociously. One by one, each species of animal released its own call into the wild. Waves protruded from the ocean wall, causing the people to instantly turn around. The sea creatures were frantically swimming upward to the surface. Hundreds of them gathered at the edge of the ocean wall looking out at the people.

"What's happening?" Deon asked.

"I've never seen this before Deon. I don't have the slightest clue," Priest Lance replied as he marveled at the sight of all the mermaids and sea creatures at the edge of the ocean wall.

In the distance behind the mermaids and sea creatures, a glowing object quickly approached. The people gasped in fear of what was coming. The closer it got, the more violent the waves became. The mermaids were as still as statues with all of their attention focused on Deon. The young man stood to his feet enchanted by the unknown. Suddenly, the glowing object became too bright for them to look at. It illuminated the entire wall causing everyone to cover their eyes.

"Deon." That voice could be heard for miles. The ground immediately stopped trembling and the ocean calmed. Before uncovering his eyes, Deon knew exactly who it was.

"Mama!" Deon screamed.

Everyone else uncovered their eyes when they heard Deon scream out to his mother. They were amazed to see him being held by a tall, beautiful woman who wore white flowing garb. She looked healthier and more beautiful than Deon had ever seen her. She held her baby tightly as tears of joy rolled down his cheeks.

"I Love you," Deon said as he hugged her tight as he could.

Love knelt down before Deon and held his hand. She had kept her promise, and Deon was elated. All of the small people looked on in awe.

"Baby, you are the most important thing that ever happened to me. You're going to grow up and be everything I could have never been. When I was telling you about this place, I didn't know it was real baby. Something in my spirit was telling me that I had to tell you something. The story I told you was so clear in my thoughts. It felt like I had been here a hundred times."

"Then how could you be sure, Mama?"

"I wasn't. I just didn't want you to hurt too bad because I was leaving. I prayed and prayed that you wouldn't have to suffer. Every single time I saw you in that facility you were smiling. But I knew you were hurting sweetie…When my daddy had to go, I hurt so badly. I didn't want you to have to carry that burden over me. God was telling me exactly how to explain it to you. I was half out of it, but when I saw that big smile, I knew you were going to be okay."

"I don't ever want to lose you again, Mama."

"You didn't lose me D. I'm going to always be with you," she said as she put her hand over Deon's heart.

"D, you're the strongest of you three. You've gotta be there for everybody. You might be the youngest, but Lexy thinks you're one of the strongest men she's ever met. And Bryce looks forward to reading those letters you send him every week. Sometimes, those letters are the only thing that helps him make it through. Grandma Minnie knows how to pray, but she wishes she could pray like you. Papa loves the ground you walk on, baby. And your dad…He can't make it without you. "

"Mama, can I stay here with you?"

"Deon, you already know that I gotta go. This place is beautiful, but ain't nothing more beautiful than where I'm going son. Deon, I want you to remember something. There's never ever going to be anything wrong with what God plans for you. Faith is what got us here right now, and the only reason you delivered those messages is because of faith. When you think about why this all happened years from now, and see the kind of mountains faith can move, you'll be able to accomplish anything you put your faith in."

"But I still don't understand why I had to tell Papa about that note and tell daddy about that red door Mama."

"Just know that God used you, Deon. There's going to be some times in life when that's the only thing that matters. Now, look me in my face and tell me that you don't want me to go on to Heaven," Love said sarcastically as she looked out of the corner of her eye to catch Deon's facial expression.

"That's crazy! I wouldn't ever tell you not to go to Heaven. That's the whole point of being a Christian. That's what Grandma always told me."

"Then you know that I have to go, and you know that you have to get back."

"So, am I ever going to see you again?"

"Not until God calls you Deon. The only way you're ever going to see me is if you make it, and you know everything you have to do to make it. Heaven is really real, baby. I know you've been wanting to know that for the longest. It really is Deon. Now you gotta hurry up and get back. They're worried sick over you."

"I'll always Love you Mama. What about this place though?" Deon asked as he looked around at all the people. Neesah, Lo, Edward, and Sterling were all standing around patiently with tears in their eyes. Priest Lance was trying his best not to cry.

"You'll always be welcome to come here Deon. You know that," Priest Lance said.

"You gotta go back now, baby," Love insisted.

"I can help him get there a little faster Ms. Love," Priest Lance said.

Love and Deon embraced one last time before he walked her to the edge of the ocean wall where the mermaids were waiting to send her off. Love kissed him on his forehead and told him that she had just given him something to remember their last meeting by. As soon as she stepped in the wall of water, she was whisked away just as quickly as she had come.

306

As they all were gathered around to wave goodbye to Love, Priest Lance dug into his pocket and pulled out another vile of the glowing liquid that Deon drank on his last visit and handed it to him. Deon took the vile from him and turned around to face the crowd.

"Thank you for going through all the trouble of planning the party, but she couldn't stay long and I gotta get back. I'll see you all soon." He gave each of his new friends a hug before drinking the liquid. He knew how light headed the potion would make him feel so he went to sit on the sand before he drank it. This time the taste was so strong it caused him to cough uncontrollably. The crowd smiled at him as he slowly drifted back to sleep. Suddenly, everything faded to black.

"Breathe slowly Deon," a voice said as he came to.

Deon woke up with an oxygen mask on in the hospital bed. He was coughing in the same manner that he had after he drank the potion out of the vile.

Mrs. Minnie, Mr. Riggs, Alexia, and Mr. Harry Lennon's parents were all in the room. The nurse removed the oxygen mask and turned Deon over on his side so that he could catch his breath.

"Praise God," Mrs. Minnie said.

"What happened?" Deon asked as his coughing slowly came to an end.

"You've been in a terrible accident Deon. But you're going to be just fine with a little rest."

"Where's my dad? Is he okay?" Deon asked.

"He's right down the hall, D. Y'all got in an accident and he lost a lot of blood. He's okay though. The doctors are just running a few more tests on him," Mr. Riggs replied.

The nurse continued to work on Deon as the family thanked God that both of them were going to be okay. They would not have been able to bear another tragedy so close to Love's death. As soon as Deon was cleaned up, a nurse and the doctor rolled Diondre into the room in a wheelchair.

"Deon! You ok son?" Diondre loudly asked. His head was bandaged up and his left leg was in a cast. He almost jumped out of the wheelchair to get to Deon when he saw that Deon was okay. Mrs. Minnie quickly went over and put her hand on his shoulder for him to sit still so that he wouldn't further injure his leg.

"He's fine Diondre. He just needs his rest," she softly said.

"Daddy, what happened? I really don't remember anything."

"I lost control of the truck and we went over into the river."

"He's got a little concussion, but he's fine. You two are extremely lucky. It could have been a lot worse from what the state trooper told me. You guys will stay here tonight, just for precaution, but will be free to go in the morning."

The doctor was able to find a double room for Diondre and Deon to stay in that night. Mrs. Minnie and Alexia stayed with the two of them. They all talked and laughed throughout the night. Mrs. Minnie enjoyed seeing how happy the children were with their father.

At one point Alexia helped Deon out of his bed so that he could go to the bathroom. He really didn't need her help getting up, but she insisted that he allow her to do what an older sister should do in times like these. After he washed his hands in the sink, he looked up at the mirror and saw a dark bruise on his forehead. He leaned closer and saw that it looked as if someone had kissed him on his forehead with dark lipstick.

"So that's what she left me," he said to himself. He couldn't help but smile at the memory of what his mother had told him.

Later that night when Deon fell asleep with his sister in the reclining chair beside him, Mrs. Minnie and Diondre stayed up watching television. Both of them looked over at the two of those children in adoration. The sight warmed their hearts.

"Diondre, those babies look just like you. Thank God you ain't ugly," Mrs. Minnie said. Both she and Diondre laughed quietly.

"Thank you Mrs. Minnie," he replied.

"Don't thank me. Thank Love for picking you," Mrs. Minnie said. As soon as she said her daughter's name, the pockets of their eyes began to fill with tears.

"Diondre, everybody has their own journey. Everybody's journey is filled with mistakes. Some more than others. But either way, the only thing that really matters at the end of the day is how you finish."

"Your Love…She finished well Diondre. I'm so proud. You see those precious babies over there. They need their daddy like they've never needed him before. You gotta get yourself together, because I can't do this alone no more, Diondre."

"I know Mrs. Minnie, but it's so hard. I promised her that that's what I'm going to do, and I ain't breaking that promise. I broke too many to her while she was here." As soon as he began to speak, the tears streamed down the sides of his face.

"Where are you going to live, Diondre? You can't keep bouncing around and staying out there in them streets. What do you think it'll do to those kids if they wake up one morning and find out that somebody found you dead out there?" Mrs. Minnie asked with concern as she wept. Diondre stared at the ceiling thinking about what he had just said.

"You coming to stay at the house. You can't get around on that leg out there by yourself. And you're going to spend some real time with those kids. We're going to figure out how to get you off that stuff, and how you can get on your feet. And I'm not asking you. I'm telling you. Love made me promise that I was going to help you get yourself together, so I'm stuck with you. She got me with her smart ass," Mrs. Minnie said as she chuckled at the end of her sentence.

"Mrs. Minnie!" Diondre said, surprised that she had cursed.

"Shut up boy. I'm grown. Now hug my neck before I start cussing some more." She leaned over and hugged Diondre.

"I'm sorry for being so mean all these years. I pray you forgive."

"I love you, Mrs. Minnie."

The next morning they all left the hospital and went to Mrs. Minnie's house. The children were overjoyed that Diondre was coming to live with them. Mr. Riggs came over and gave Diondre a ride to get all of his belongings. While they were out, Deon and Alexia prepared Bryce's old room so their father could have a place to sleep. Mrs. Minnie made the final arrangements for Love's funeral. The entire family had dinner together that night, including Mr. Harry Lennon's parents. It was wonderful to see everyone together fellowshipping as a tight knit family should.

Diondre put Deon to bed each night, and spent quality time with him and his sister for the following two days. Mrs. Minnie was a little jealous at all the attention they were giving Diondre, but she was glad that they were happy.

On the day of the funeral, they all ate breakfast together. Shortly after, the entire family gathered at Mrs. Minnie's house to wait on the two limousines that would carry them to the funeral. When Pastor Williams arrived, he led the family in a short prayer. He was a little surprised at how much happier this family seemed in comparison to others he had spent time with before a funeral.

"This family is so blessed. God brought y'all comfort a long time ago," he said as he stood before them after the prayer. Shortly after, they lay Love to rest. Every last one of them smiled as they thought about the wonderful person Love had transformed into before she passed.

Love's funeral, just like her father's, was held at the auditorium at Southeastern Community College. There were almost as many people there as there were for Mr. Harry Lennon's funeral. After all, she was his daughter. As they pulled in front of the building, Deon screamed in excitement.

"Look. There's Bryce!"

Bryce stood at the door with two prison guards who were escorting him. He looked like he had lost a lot of weight. He was wearing a simple white button up with a pair of black pants. As Pastor Williams led the family towards the door, the guards took the handcuffs off his wrists. He hugged each of them with tears in his eyes, and told them he was sorry. Everyone was so happy to see him. Deon wouldn't let Bryce go. The sight made all of them smile, even the guards. One of the guards had to be by him at all times, so they allowed Deon to be the last one in line as they entered into the auditorium so that he could sit by his older brother.

As they sat in the first two rows at the front of the auditorium, they saw just how much Love was loved. It seemed like all of the residents of Whiteville were there. Her neighbors from the projects, previous co-workers, drug dealers, countless friends and many family members sat there proudly. Even Kye and

Sarah came from the facility to the funeral service. There was not one open seat left in the auditorium.

As the ceremony went on, the family smiled through all of their tears. Deon, however, didn't shed one tear. He was holding on tightly to what his mother told him. He was at peace. And soon all the rest of his family would be at peace too.

When Pastor Williams stood up to give Love's eulogy, he was encouraged by all of the smiling faces in the crowd.

"I had this whole thing geared for a sad crowd of people, hurt because God called one of his angels home. Well, y'all done messed that up," Pastor Williams said jokingly. The entire room started laughing.

"She knew me when they called me 'Smiley'…"

From that point on, Pastor Williams candidly told stories of how Love emphasized the importance of having a relationship with God regardless of the struggles a person wrestled with.

As he preached, Bryce reached in his shirt pocket and pulled out a folded sheet of paper. The guard looked a little worried at first, but then calmed down after Bryce whispered something to him. He nudged Deon and gave it to him. Deon looked up at him a little confused as he unfolded the paper. When he opened it up and saw what it was, his eyes widened. After Deon sent Bryce that last letter about the place he saw in his dreams, Bryce drew it for him just as detailed as he had described it. Deon folded the paper and put it away in his suit pocket. It would be something that he cherished for the rest of his life.

At the end of the ceremony, each of them took a final look at Love before they closed the casket. She was as beautiful as ever, and could finally rest peacefully. After they closed the casket, they then made their way to her burial location. She would be buried right next to her father. As soon as they began lowering her body into the ground, it rained. They believed that the rain was always a sign that whoever was being buried would go to Heaven. It brought a smile to all of their faces.

As they stood there watching them lower Love into the ground, Deon saw the strangest thing as he looked up and around at the crowd. Right across from him in the group of people that were standing on the other side of the grave, was a short man in a suit accompanied by a beautiful young girl. As he focused his eyes to look closer, they disappeared into a group of people that were leaving. He could have sworn that he had just seen Priest Lance and Neesah.

After Love was buried, they stood around and said their goodbyes to Bryce before he had to leave with the guards. He promised them all that he was going to write and call at least once a week until he was released and place all of their names on the list so that they could visit him. When they parted ways, tons of people came by Mrs. Minnie's to comfort the family during their time of grief. It turned out to be a beautiful celebration of Love's life. Mrs. Minnie knew that she and her family would be fine as long as they had each other.

# Epilogue

After failing many times before, Diondre successfully completed the drug rehabilitation program that Mrs. Minnie sent him to. Mrs. Minnie was able to convince the supervisor at Marley's Insurance Company to hire him. Everyone in town was so proud of him that they couldn't resist changing their insurance policies to one of the many great plans he was offering. Before long, he had bought himself a car and moved him and his children into a nice home in the middle of town. Deon started attending public school and Alexia had drastically improved her grades. They were truly happy.

As for the rest of the family, Mrs. Minnie found love after all those years alone. She would come by and visit the children almost every day, but on the weekends, she and her new sweetheart would spend most of their time together. The family adored him and was so glad that she had found happiness again.

Mr. Riggs finally built up the courage to go overseas on an airplane. Alexia would get online and plan his two-week long vacations that he would take every other month. He had more money than he knew what to do with and was finally taking an opportunity to see the world in his old age. He was having the time of his life.

Mr. Harry Lennon's parents continued to travel as they always had, and made sure that they ate dinner at Mrs. Minnie's house at least one Sunday out of the month. Some Sundays, they would all go to the prison to visit Bryce.

One Sunday as they all were eating dinner at Mrs. Minnie's, there was a loud knock at the door that startled everyone. Deon ran quickly to open the door and found Ryan Roseboro standing on the porch with the biggest smile Deon had ever seen.

"Hey Deon, is your grandmother home?" he eagerly asked.

"She's right in there. Come on in."

When Ryan walked into the kitchen where everyone was sitting, they knew that he had great news.

"Hey y'all. I'm glad everyone is here. I've got some news that's going to blow you away," Ryan said excitingly as he stood in the doorway.

"I just got a call from the D.A a little while ago. How about Lil' Ms. Lisa Taylor got herself arrested last night for being drunk as a dog at a party at the American Legion Hut. She was drunk and high as a kite on everything."

"We don't care nothing about that chick, Mr. Roseboro!" Alexia asserted.

"I aint finished," he replied excitedly

"While they were booking her she started blabbing off at the mouth about how her dad was going to get her out, and they couldn't do nothing to her. And then she started talkin' 'bout how she got Bryce locked up. The officer booking her was the same one that booked Bryce that night, and so he

321

started prying about what really happened. She told him everything!"

"So what does that mean?" Mrs. Minnie asked with a confused look on her face.

"That means that a whole bunch of those charges are about to get dropped tomorrow morning. He's still gotta do some time, but his time is about to get cut a whole lot shorter. If we can work this thing right, he'll be home by the end of next year."

"Praise God!" Mrs. Minnie screamed. That was one of the happiest days they had seen in a while. It was only a matter of time before they would all be together again.

Deon never visited that place in his dreams again, but he carried the memory of it with him each day of his life. So, does God still answer the prayers we prayed before we die? Or do those prayers even matter anymore? The truth is that every prayer matters to God. Keep praying and have faith in Him until He has you join Him in Heaven.

The End

CPSIA information can be obtained
at www.ICGtesting.com
Printed in the USA
FFOW03n0347170116
20338FF